Demise of the Mystics

ISBN: 978-1-950255-16-0

Wordbound Media
Santa Fe, NM

MAGNIFICAT
A Novel in Four Parts

Part Three:

Demise of the Mystics

Robert Stefanotti

1

$\mathcal{T}$here are times in one's life when it is necessary to retreat. For Father Brocard Connors, this was definitely one of them. Truth was, he was becoming far too notorious for a priest, and a monk at that. If you want to survive in the Church these days, don't get your name in the press for any reason whatsoever. Good or bad. Which, despite his best intentions, had hardly been the case with Brocard.

In almost as many years, he had helped solve and been responsible for the retrieval of a cache of Poussin paintings and one of the most sought after Caravaggios ever to make it to Interpol's prestigious list of Most Wanted Paintings. As if this weren't enough, he and his cohorts had exposed deep-seated corruption both in a religious community and privatized jails. With such an impressive track record, you would think that Brocard would have been publicly thanked rather than castigated, embraced rather than shunned. The problem, as it is so often the case in life, was not his deeds but the company he kept. In a word: Zinka.

Of course, a monk having a transsexual as a partner in crime would in itself be suspect. But Zinka, being Zinka, was so demonstrative that she could not help but press Brocard's frail little body up against her ample bosoms and smack a sloppy kiss on his tonsured head during the numerous press conferences and interviews they were asked to give after the solving of each of these high profile heists. Each time he caught this on the evening news, the bishop and many of the more conservative members of his flock assumed postures of pious affront as amused as they might silently have been.

For all these reasons, and for some personal ones known to Brocard alone, he had jumped at the opportunity to be Chaplain at the Mount Olivet Academy for Women. The Mount, as it was commonly called, was a rather ostentatious yet orderly academic institution with far more social than academic pretenses. Run by the remnant of a community of sisters who had lost track of their religious roots along with their habits decades before, it was a perfect place to bide his time until something more interesting came up. Which, he had no doubt, would.

The Mount also encouraged him to wear his religious habit again, something, which his recent stint as a prison chaplain, had frowned upon as unprofessional. The sisters saw it as a quaintly 'Catholic' touch to a College which had become increasingly secular. To a nun, they all gave him that 'better-you-than-me' smile of approval when he passed by. And as for the co-eds, he fit in just perfectly with the wainscoting in Taylor Hall or when seen against the flocked wallpaper in the foyer of Chandler. Blind to such concerns, Brocard clung onto his brown cowled habit as a way to connect with his past, to his years in Rome and to that commitment he had made and still kept to an Order which had seen better days. It was, quite simply, a visual metaphor for who he was: traditional, a team player and just slightly rumpled.

Not two weeks into his newfound quiet, Brocard was presented with a situation which, if not terribly unsettling, gave him cause for concern. One of the brightest and most strong-willed students, Judy McCabe, asked if he would be the advisor for her senior thesis. Her reason for asking Brocard, even though he was technically not on faculty and needed permission to cross the line from sacraments to seminar, was that her topic was caught up in issues of religious hierarchy and piety. Two things she rightfully thought he knew much about. As her family had money and contacts she had every reason to believe that she could get her project published. Similarly, there was a distinct possibility that readers might be found, given her unapologetically feminist retrieval of that controversial historic figure of Madame Guyon.

Her thesis was simply: the Catholic Church's suppression of the purported mystic Madame Guyon was not only a death knell to women in the Church but cast as suspect all mystical experiences in the Church from the seventeenth century to our present day. Now, given the grief he had just been given, was this really something which Father Brocard wanted to have his name attached to? Or for that matter, even be concerned with?

But no less a personage than Sister Colette, President of the Mount, had impressed on him the importance of taking on this project. Mr. McCabe, Judy's father, had promised to build an extension on the library. Not to mention the fact that he bankrolls the La Crosse team. There was no way out.

So it was that Brocard was found making himself as comfortable as possible — feet up on the ottoman, pot of tea at the ready on the end table — so that he could take up the challenge of critiquing Judy McCabe's project. At the very least, he thought, it might open his mind to something new — always a pleasant prospect. The presentation was good too, a rather nice cover page and clear typeface. And there was something about the title that beguiled him: *Demise of the Mystics*. A bit grand, assuredly, but then again so was the topic. At least this has nothing to do with Zinka. Or so he foolishly thought.

2

Ten years after the birth of Louis XIV and the year before Charles I of England lost his head, the woman destined to be known simply as Madame Guyon, Jeanne-Marie Bouvier de la Mothe, was born. It is a name that conjures up degenerate hysteria to the French; and yet that same name often rouses deep admiration in Germany and England. Of all stories, hers cannot be told dispassionately, no less objectively. But in its tragic sweep and bizarre turns, it perfectly frames the frenzied demise of the mystics.

A rather snappy start, Brocard thought, as he took a sip of tea and paused for a moment to admire the flame of the candle burning on the end table. Vanilla. Something he picked up from Zinka and about which he got no end of grief from the Pastor of the rectory where he had been living before moving into rooms at the Mount. Fruity, he said. Well, maybe it was, but he liked it, plain and simple. And what's wrong with fruits? But, back to the text.

She was the first daughter of the second marriage of the notably pious Claude Bouvier, Seigneur de la Mothe-Vergonville, Procurator of the King of France, as well connected, as he was rich.

Now that will definitely not do. Circling the suspect

sentence for editing, Brocard rushed ahead, to see what she was trying to say. "Madame Guyon, as she would later be known," he scrawled in the margins, "was part of her father's second family. And a considerably small part of it. Her older brother Jacques, it seems, got all the attention. As did the four children from the first marriage, all of whom were sent on to the priesthood or religious life. Little Jeanne-Marie, being a girl and sickly at that, was barely tolerated."

As he strained more tea into his cup, an image of a Jansenistic couple, Catholic Puritans if you will, flashed before Brocard's eyes. He did not have to read the text to know how bizarre their behavior was. Underneath their ruffled collars and thick wool jackets, small hooks ripped into their flesh. Scabs formed and were reopened with every measured move they took. They were breakfasting standing up, as Brocard had done as a novice three centuries after them, so that they would take no pleasure in the food that they were eating. Would not linger over earthly delights, like the *massa damnata*, the unchosen. This was the couple that bred and raised the mystic who was destined to bring the whole panoply of religion down.

> *Jeanne-Marie had the most horrid of childhoods. When she was two she was put into an Ursuline Convent, the superior of which was a relative. However, for health reasons she had to be sent home where she was put under the care of domestics. Then, when she was four, she was sent to a Benedictine Convent, under the patronage of the Duchess of Montblazon, a friend of her fathers. Again, her continuing frail health forced her to leave. Finally in 1655, ostensibly because of his concern for her education, her father put her under the care of her step-sister, Marie de Sainte-Cecile Bouvier, an Ursuline sister and a friend of St. Jane de Chantal (companion of that summit of Christian compassion, St. Francis de Sales). She provided the nearest approximation to love the young girl was ever to know.*

How strange, he thought as he looked back into the flame and took a deep breath of vanilla, how strange this dressing up of children like little nuns and monks. At least he was fifteen when he went into his religious order. Advanced in years by little Jeanne-Marie's standards, but admittedly still embarrassingly young by modern standards. He remembered still the coarse fabric of his first religious habit rubbing against skin that was too young, too translucent and too sensitive to endure it. And in a strange way, he felt what it was like for this child nun to be bound up and trotted out, made to sit on cold, uninviting choir stalls for hours of every day. Yet feeling, as Brocard himself had done, that there was at least somewhere she belonged. Somewhere where her presence was not resented, or worse still, unnoticed.

But it seems that after spending only three years there, the great spiritual progress the young girl was making made another one of her stepsisters in the convent jealous. Her father had Jeanne-Marie, who by this time was used to disappointments, put under the care of another friend, the prioress of a nearby Dominican convent. Here she came down with the smallpox and went temporarily blind. She would continue to have problems with her eyes throughout her life. Forced to return home again at ten, she lived the life of an exclaustrated nun.

The word 'exclaustrated', so unexpected on the pen of an American undergraduate, brought a smile to Brocard's lips. That was, of course, his lifestyle. Living outside the monastery. But in his case, it was less because of health than because the monastery had collapsed into a pile of rubble. Poor San Redempto, home for more years than he cared to remember. Then again, he chose not to move into one of his religious community's remaining monasteries. He needed a break from all the demands which a group of bachelors, no matter how well intentioned or even spiritual, invariably make.

In throwing herself into her devotions and readings, she could temporarily avoid her increasingly unpleasant mother. As was the fashion of the day for young girls, she devoted long periods of time to spiritual reading. The book which held the greatest sway over her was Henri de Maupas' The Life of Jane de Chantal, on whom she consciously began to model herself. Finally, she longed to go into the convent, to become a Visitation sister, the group of nun's founded by St. Jane. But, wouldn't you know it, this did not fit her parents' plans.

"Wouldn't you know it?" Wouldn't you know it? He reached over for the red pen, nearly knocking over the teapot in his desire to excise the Valley-speak from an otherwise competent exposition. Wouldn't you know it? Brocard's eyes ran down the page, careening into facts and images, in an attempt to guard against any similar grammatical gaffs. The flickering light of the candle gave life to the page. Image rushed on image as he saw, literally saw young Jeanne-Marie, pockmarked face and squinting eyes, tending her bedridden father. Morning, afternoon and evening answering the call of his bell, with food trays and cold compresses. There were servants who could have done all this and more, but in his tyrannical wisdom, her father saw this as her duty, and hers alone. Then, barely clinging onto life, he made one final decision for his daughter—a decision that would rid him and his estate of any additional obligation for the child he seemed to have wished he never had. At age fifteen, it was announced that she was to be married to Jacques Guyon within the month. Money alone recommended him.

What a horrid, twisted face he had. Even though Brocard knew that he was an invalid and over two decades older than Jeanne-Marie, he was revolted by his sallow skin, pinched features and sanctimonious bearing. Before Jeanne-Marie turned sixteen not only was she encumbered with this horror, but also her sister, Marie de Sainte-Cecile, the Ursuline nun with whom she lived almost as a daughter, passed away. Loss upon loss. And things were not to get better.

During the twelve years of their loveless marriage, Madame Guyon gave birth to five children. Typical of the brutality of the period, even for the very rich, only three, two boys and a girl, survived their childhood.

Why is it, Brocard wondered, that piety—saintly or

10

skewed—always needs hardship as soil in which to grow? And what was it about this story, this period, this woman that was beginning to grip him? As if some splinter of her soul was lodged in his. As if it had something to tell him which he had to hear.

There were two simple answers, he thought, as he finished off his tea and made his way over to the computer. Either he was certifiably crazy, a distinct possibility he had to admit; or, the story of Madame Guyon was triggering something in him for a purpose. He knew already that it was time for him to contact his old friend and confidant—the only person who could help him sort out the sane from the delusional. So he logged on to his computer and dove into cyberspace, in quest of an answer to the past, which might well prove to be his future.

3

*F*ather Avertanus was still not dead, which perplexed his superiors no end. He had been moved up to Zenderen, where the community sent its chronically ill and aged to die comfortably, nearly two years ago. Quite truthfully, he had outlived his welcome. Not that they were pushing death any more aggressively in his case than in others. But they were Dutch after all—the country that embraces giving that added push to those that death does not take in speedy fashion. It's such a small country; everyone must do one's part. Not excluding dying.

His religious community had assigned him to a lovely room overlooking their undeniably festive cemetery where he was to be lodged until the resurrection of the body. Surrounded by herbaceous borders and covered by colorful annuals swaying with military precision in the springtime breeze, it was the most tempting of steps for an ancient man with numerous infirmities to take. To all, that is, except Avertanus—one of those men of faith who, while never doubting the reward to come, was in no way eager to claim it. Life in the here and now was simply too amusing and gloriously unpredictable to abandon to blissful surety. As the convoluted email he had just received from Father Brocard so beautifully illustrated:

11

My dear, dear friend and sometime mentor,

I need your advice. Is it possible to break down the boundaries between time and space and be in another place and time? More to the point, in someone else's life? How strange that must sound; yet, how serious the question.

I think I might do well to back up for a bit. To explain this outburst — which as you well know, is alien to my normal, rather ponderous way of communicating. Where to begin?

You know I have recently taken on the position of chaplain at a twee girls' college where I had hoped anything momentous would pass me by. Which indeed was the case until I was asked to advise one of the brighter seniors on her final project: Demise of the Mystics, a study of Madame Guyon. Yes, one and the same — the bizarre heretic. It seems she enjoys newfound fame as a post-feminist martyr. Surely one of the perversities of revisionist history but that is not the issue that concerns me.

While I was reading the opening chapters I found myself caught up in ways that far exceeded academic interest or even empathy. (The latter I had to say, as there are parts of her early life that resonate deeply with my own). There were times that my eyes would leave the page and, in the flicker of the candle on my end table, I saw the young Mlle. Marie herself. And not only saw her, but heard rustling of the nuns' habits as they made their way to prayer, even smelt those undisguised earthly odors which set the seventeenth century apart from our overly sanitized time.

Tell me my mind is overactive, please. Or that I am becoming delusional in my old age. Anything else would be far too fearsome.

Awaiting your reply, I remain, your friend — Brocard.

The candle, of course, was the key and justifiable reason for his fear. But how would poor Brocard have known that such a simple devise could render such results? That such a seemingly innocuous decorating touch could, given the right circumstances and combination of historic and present day persons, be transformed into a virtual time-machine.

In order to confirm his suspicions he had to find the descriptive passage in Albertus Magnus, the incunabula on alchemy, which he alone had rights to read in the community. It was rightfully *disciplina arcana*, hidden wisdom, which, in the wrong hands might be abused.

Energized by the thought of his friend in Pennsylvania having access to the Golden Age of French spirituality, even at its most suspect, Avertanus pulled the cowl over his head against the morning dampness and made his way down to the library. Distressed as Brocard himself might be by what was happening, Avertanus had no doubt that he could calm him down. That in fact he could make him embrace this new reality as the gift that it was. This was not the first time in his life when he had been called on to calm his brother's jitters. Nor would it be the last.

First he had to assure that this was no mere coincidence and that, more importantly, this state could be summonsed at will. Casting an eye down at the cemetery as he made his way along the darkened clerestory, he could only smile at death. Not now. Have patience. There's work to be done.

4

$\mathcal{D}$oesn't everyone long to know where they come from? Not just the womb that bore them — although for many that would be an absolute treat — but the blood which courses through their bodies, the cultural memory that fires the synapses in their brain and the genetic quirks that make them who they are. Finding a coat of arms would be pleasant, but not necessary. No, Zinka thought as she gazed out the train window at the Slovenian countryside rolling by, one perverted noble ancestor would be enough to explain her to herself. One measly cross-dressing Earl, one butch chatelaine would be quite enough to connect her to that sweep of human history from which she had been cut-off for a lifetime.

Objectively speaking, it was not easy being Zinka. The hair alone, piled mightily on top of her head, required endless attention. Not to mention the nails filed down and pointed so as to distract from her gargantuan hands; the spiked heels which wore down quicker than you could whistle under the weight of her bulk — all these took time and trouble. Perhaps if she had been born a woman (or at least with all of the anatomical parts in place because her heart was always on the distaff side) she might not have been so driven. As it was, hers was the manic faith of a convert, which did not allow her a moment's rest in pursuit of being *femina* herself — the perfect dame.

Fame as well had come to her late in life. Well, not that late, as she looked far younger than her years. All that could be said of her is that she was a woman of a certain age. Like much else, facts were not what Zinka was about — until of course the press got involved. Where exactly are your from? What is that accent? Is it true you were a sergeant in the Yugoslav army? Answers had to be given, now that she had become such a famous art-historian sleuth. Her public demanded to know. And, what was more troubling to her still — as this was a sentiment that had never reared its head before — was that she too needed some answers. Perhaps, she thought, studying herself in the reflection of the train window as it became opaque under the shadow of overhanging trees, perhaps she was getting old. Then a smile came across her face as she saw just how radiant she looked, how young and beguiling. No, she was just curious.

To make a long and tortuous story more bearable, here were the details: born, Milorad Pavlik, into a Croatian and very Catholic family, she (then he) became attracted to the toughness of the Serbs and after gymnasium (or high school if you will) moved to Belgrade to pursue his studies. This was just the first of a series of breaks from his past, in an attempt to re-invent himself. His years in the military during the halcyon years of Marshal Tito not only brought him to the rank of sergeant but also to the awareness that the pants did not fit him well. He became convinced that not only did the clothes have to go, but also the anatomical parts. They quite clearly were holding him back from being who he really was. Which was, given his inordinate fondness of the opera diva Zinka Milanov: Zinka. Years went by before the change was complete. There was counseling to be done and hormones to be taken. As the breasts expanded so too did his mind. Physical transformation marched in tandem with doctoral studies, until, finally, Dr. Zinka Pavlik — as sexy as she was brainy — burst onto the scene. What was left behind, what had to be abandoned to her singular determination, were the roots, the culture and family — anything in fact that might distract.

In truth, Milorad aka Zinka had never been close to her family. They understood her even less than she understood herself. So that the news that her mother's body had given way to obesity or that her father had been impaled through the left eye by a steel rod at work, caused her to skip a heartbeat. Little more. She did have a sister, though, who she remembered as a sympathetic creature, starry eyed and frail. It was in pursuit of Natalia that she had set out on her journey north to Vienna.

Whether or not she would even be at the address she was given was not certain. One of the Pavliks' old neighbors, to whom Zinka identified herself as no one more than a friend of the family, said that all of them were dead or had long since left Slovenia. Natalia, it seems, had come back once to visit, rather grandly dressed for a village girl they all knew when, and had left her business card.

The sweat from Zinka's palm was making the print run, but not enough that the words didn't sing out to her with ominous promise: High Priestess Natalia Pavlik, Psychic Channel to the Age of Doom. As the train approached Vienna, so too did her anticipation. And dread.

5

A bolt of lightening surged through her body causing it to jolt violently into her chair, blinding her with light too bright for human eyes to see. It was God, quite clearly God, but the effect was radically physical. Were it not for the priest kneeling in front of her distended body, Brocard would have offered her assistance. As it was, he could only watch and be caught up in the unbridled emotions of the moment.

"*Ouvrez les bras!*" he encouraged her with the most earnest of voices. "Open your arms to God, the Light of All!" At which, Madame Guyon's arms flung open and clipping Père Bertot on the head knocked him on his ass. How elegantly he tumbled though.

No rough edges were to be found on this prelate—bewigged and perfumed and decked out in the most beautifully tailored of suits. True, there was an austerity about him, but like all things Jansenist, this too was aristocratic in tone.

"*Viens! Viens mon Époux!*" Yes, her True Spouse, Jesus, not that shriveled up invalid she had been forced to marry, but Jesus, Himself, had taken her. And she longed to have Him penetrate her, rip her apart with His presence, spurt His life into her and her alone. "Come!" she murmured pulling the scarf from around her neck to reveal a plunging décolleté. "Come!" she moaned over and over again beseechingly.

Both of the good Fathers, the Père at her feet and Brocard, feeling more and more like a voyeur pressed up in the corner of the room, didn't know where to look first. With her hair loosened and cascading down to her shoulders her face was framed in auburn waves, heightening the radiance of her skin and the lusciousness of her parted lips. Then there were her delicate hands, with the most beautifully manicured nails, wiggling about in the air like a veritable Dance of Shiva. Finally—oh where to look first—there were her quite enormous breasts, made larger still by her diminutive size, which heaved to get out of her bustier under the power of the spirit. Actually, there was no contest: the breasts won.

Could any twenty-year old, not just in 1668 but at any time, have been more captivating? Surely, Père Bertot had never known anyone to rival her, and he moved in the most aesthetically elevated of circles. None of the courtesan's who had their carriages driven brazenly in the Bois de Boulogne at sunset, and who the devil had set to torment him on numerous occasions, none of them could hold a candle to this vibrant wife of Monsignor Jacques Guyon. None were more desirable than this woman God himself had clearly chosen to penetrate before his very eyes.

The smells in the closed room were overwhelming. It was not just the sweat that poured out of the mystic and her admirers, an understandable consequence of a July afternoon in Paris, but the inordinate amount of pheromones as well. The air was quite simply charged with sex. Madame Guyon was experiencing the release she had longed for; Père Bertot was smitten by a love that he had never thought possible. And as for Brocard, he was wondering what he had gotten into.

6

*H*e could see no reason why he shouldn't forward her email to Brocard. After all, it was quite clear to Avertanus that he was just being used as a go-between. It was Brocard, not him, to whom she really wanted to pour out her soul. Or zeitgeist at least — as 'soul' seemed too tame a word for the inner workings of Zinka. This is what she wrote:

My dearest Avertanus it has been too long as well since I've seen or even heard from you or my little pumpkin Brocard. I do cause him so much grief. Too much needless anxiety. Especially as there is no crime to be stopped or artwork to be found. How I long to work with my blushing little monk again, but I don't want to get the bishop in a tizzy, you know. Far be it from me, innocent little waif that I am. Well, big waif, perhaps. But waif nevertheless and that's my reason for intruding on your monastic solitude. Cutting to the chase, wise old monk, I am in search of my roots. Well, not all of them admittedly but at least something to tell me what and whom I am connected to. Hard as it might be to believe this, I have become rather untethered these past few decades. You know, like those Macy's balloons in that splendid Thanksgiving Day Parade those Americans have. A large breasted woman hovering over Broadway, being buffeted by the winds, desperate to be anchored down if not deflated. Well, you get my drift. Anyway, that is my reason for being in Vienna, where I find myself in the most perplexing of situations. You see, I've located my sister, the only relative living or dead who remotely interests me to contact, and she's as suspect as she is crazy. Or so it seems to me at this distance.

The address I had been given for her, where once it seems she gave psychic readings or something of the sort, is now an information center for the commune that she has founded. It's a rather tasteful establishment I must say — a large storefront inside the Ring with subtle lighting, leather armchairs. On the wall is the most amusing image of a woman breastfeeding an older man in the Latin Charity trope, which I'm sure you remember from your years in Rome as it was a favorite image of the baroque. You know, girl with engorged breasts feeding her starving father in jail. Prurient to be sure, yet spiritual in its own delightful way.

Anyway, Natalia, my sister, the High Priestess no less of the Divine Children of Lactation – no, my dear, I could not make this one up – is no longer based in Vienna but, it seems, only recruits there. A booking office for retreats or, as she calls them, 'experiences' at their compound just outside Prague in the Czech countryside. Seems quite a lovely place, although God-only-knows what awaits me there. You see, I am going out there but, and this is my reason for writing, I am reluctant to come right out and tell Natalia it is her long lost brother. After all with tits like these, she's hardly going to jump to that conclusion. Awaiting your advice, I remain,

Your loving little Zinka

As if Zinka would or could ever wait for advice in anything.

7

*T*here was little consolation in his words. In fact, it seemed to Father Brocard that his old friend Avertanus was reveling in these uninvited experiences to which he was being subjugated, rather than showing him a way out. Combing through the archives at Zenderen, Avertanus had retrieved the *Alchemical Ritual of Bihabitation,* or living with and in another time and place. Using the candle as a locus, Avertanus had encouraged Brocard to repeat an incantation which would allow him to control, as best one could, his moving back into the seventeenth century of Madame Guyon. Without this devise, Avertanus warned, an abrupt and even violent seizing might occur, causing lasting psychological harm. With it, as Avertanus said with unusual candor, he could relax and enjoy the show.

There was one other way out. Namely, give the document back to Judy McCabe and tell her that he could not help her. But what excuse could he rationally give? Surely no one would believe the truth (they rarely do in life at best of times). It was inconceivable that he, an academically trained monk, would not be the best person on campus to advise such a project. Nor would it be wise to risk offending one of the college's major benefactors, as Judy's father was. No, there was no way out except going deeper into it all.

There was no denying the fact that Brocard was gaining a deeper understanding of the period and person of Madame Guyon than any senior paper, indeed any book, could ever render. The snag here was he was seeing things that explained situations for which there was no documentation. Take Madame Guyon's persistent eye problems as an example. The paper read:

> In 1671, when Père Bertot had moved back up to Paris, she used the pretext that she had to go to Paris to have her chronically weak eyes seen to.

Did Judy even know what she had written? Could she have even known that Père Bertot left the convent in the country where he had been doing spiritual direction precisely because he was so dangerously attracted to this young, married woman? And could she even have imagined, as Brocard had witnessed, that she would run off to Paris after him because of her need? Not for him physically — those needs were beautifully seen to by the Lord — but for his adulation. The way in which Bertot worshipped her alone. That was the need which was growing in her and which could not be sated.

Brocard knew that he had to discuss this with Judy — it was time anyway that he sit down with her and discuss the paper — but wondered how he could begin to broach such sensitive, not to say arcane, topics. However as she bounded into his office, overflowing with that hormone-driven energy of youth, he realized he had to do little more than sit back and reflect how best to respond. He was always more comfortable following when some one else led. In this dance, Judy McCabe did not disappoint.

"I'm dying to know what you think? Terrific, isn't it? Terrific." Obviously this young woman's self-esteem was in good working order. So much so in fact that, except for noticing that

19

Father Brocard was signaling her to take a chair, nothing else mattered except the words that simply had to come tumbling out. It was so clear to Judy, so blindingly clear, that her work on Madame Guyon was as academically important as it was riveting to read. All that the book—it was a book in her mind and not a student paper—needed was a little polishing up. Something she felt that Brocard could do.

"I just can't believe how they got it all wrong, you know? I mean, for centuries, the way all those men," she gave a coquettish stress to this word for Brocard's benefit, "couldn't handle her power. You know, like the way she had this direct channel to God? Did you get to the channeling sections yet? Like, you know, she was a seventeenth century Shirley MacLane."

"I haven't arrived to that point of your paper." How could someone whose verbal communication was scarred by Valley-speak write as well as she did? Not waiting to find out, he blurted out his question. "Does your research show that Guyon manipulated religion to control others?"

Perplexed that such a question should even be asked, Judy replied quite simply, "Religion, sex, power—whatever—it's all the same, right?"

8

*T*he mystery of the moment, perverse as it might be, entranced her. If painted by Artemesia, it would have doubtless enthralled thousands, indeed millions, over the years. As it was, there were less than fifty initiates witnessing this extraordinary scene. And Zinka, as well—not fully an initiate yet, but sorely tempted to be one.

The 'Temple' they were gathered in had been the dining hall in the Medieval castle taken over by the religious commune. Rays of light flooded in from clear, high windows, casting deep shadows on everyone and everything within—dramatic lighting that would have gladdened the heart of Caravaggio himself. The room itself was drained of color, from the grey stone of the walls to the bleached wood of the floor, including the worshipers who were clothed in faun-coloured tunics. Everything, that is, except the woman on the altar before them: Zinka's little sister Natalia, transformed.

She was seated on an elaborate throne that had been secured to the top of the altar; and over her lap a shelf had been constructed strong enough to hold a man of any weight. On either side of the altar were burning braziers, whose flames activated the most alluring of incense, the smell of which enveloped the temple. The High Priestess Natalia herself, draped in crimson red chiffon, sat transfixed as a man of indeterminate age, body curled in foetal position, lay on the shelf above her lap and suckled her breast.

The sacramentality of this act — for it purported to be no less, nor did any of the worshipers view it as less than sacred — was underscored by the chant taken up by the congregation: *Veni Creator Spiritu*, Come Creating Spirit. What at first had seemed to Zinka nothing short of a sacrilege was, under the sway of the moment, deeply sacred and right. Oh sister, she thought lovingly as the man's lips left her nipple and milk spurted liberally into the air, oh sister what tits you have. So life giving and perfect.

It was sometime after the service was over that Zinka finally decided it was time to leave. The temple had long since been emptied, still she found it hard to move. The worshippers had called Natalia the Lactating Virgin, a clear reference to her of that notorious way of depicting the Virgin Mary, so popular in the Baroque period, as giving milk (or was that grace?) to all who came to her breasts. In fact, there were several paintings of this curious devotion throughout the castle, not just St. Bernard the common recipient of such favors, but men and women, young and old as well. Paintings that had rarely made it into the monographs but quite authentic.

On her way back to her cell, she was so distracted that she tripped over a body — the first of several corpses that were to confound her stay.

 $\mathcal{T}$ here are those people who are constitutionally suited for the country: self-reliant souls who need fresh air and simple pleasures. Time perhaps to build a relationship or finish reading Trollop. But Bertie was not one of them. In fact, as he sat up in his cabin high in the mountains of the Abruzzi, cataloguing mushrooms and obsessing over Pino, the love of his life, he was going quietly and steadily mad.

Not that he missed being a priest, no he was well out of that; nor, for that matter, his old religious community — crazy old Avertanus and prudish Brocard, benign souls that he gave hardly a thought to anymore. But Rome — the noise and smell of the city, the bustling crowds — Rome he missed.

What made him feel even more trapped was that Pino did not feel the same. How could he, really, being a country boy himself who had tired of hustling his butt — salable though it still was — on the *Piazza della Republica*.

That is why Bertie was beside himself with glee when he heard from Zinka. He had long since gotten over her lustful ways with his boyfriend — who, after all, hadn't slept with Pino? What he remembered about Zinka even more than those fabulous heels, which he always envied, was her zest for living, her irrepressible ways. Something that had sadly gone dormant in him.

Bertie pulled her email up on the screen to give it one more read:

Carissimo Father Bertie,

It's me Zinka, crashing back into your life with a teeny-weeny favor to ask. You see, I've just found a freshly dead body that has subsequently vanished and, well, I have no one else to turn to but you to help me solve this little mystery. Brocard, you see, cannot be troubled as he is hiding out from the press, his bishop and maybe even himself at this juncture. Be that as it may. Everyone has to lead their lives as they see best. A motto I take to heart frequently in my own life, as you well know. Speaking of which, does your beauteous boyfriend still have the hardest cock this side of Tijuana? A rhetorical question, really, but if you do care to answer, be my guest. Anyway, my little melon, here's my predicament: I have gone in search of my identity, keep your comments to yourself please, and have ended up at a New Age Commune outside Prague whose guru is none other than my baby sister Natalia. Quite a charmer as the case may be, with breasts almost as ample as mine but, as you might expect of a woman from birth, quite real. Coming out of the service this afternoon in which Natalia breast-feeds select, one might say privileged, members of her community I was returning to my room when, boom, as the inmates in that jail I worked at last would say, boom, I fell flat on my derrière. It seems I had tripped on the corpse whose face was contorted in the most ghastly fashion.

Needless to say I was concerned, not to say intrigued, by my find and hastened off to find someone to report it to. The commune is in a rather grim medieval castle and, as you might expect, as quiet as a tomb. It took some time for me to locate one of the permanent residents and lead her back to the corpse, explaining in my usual animated way what I had found. Well, when we got there, you guessed it, there was no trace of the body, nor, for that matter, that there had even been a body lying there.

Now dead bodies do not simply disappear of their own accord, do they? I do not suspect, I know that there is something amiss in this paradise. My problem is, I do not feel competent to solve this by myself. For starters, as compelling as the thought of becoming an initiate is to me, can I suck my own sister's tit without it being incest? Even beyond this, my little pumpkin, four or better still six eyes are definitely better than two and, well, I simply am a team player and work better joined to others. Which does not mean that I am looking to get your boyfriend up my bum again, intriguing as that thought might be. What do you think? Can you come up to the Czech Republic for a few weeks. We could all have such fun –and might even solve a mystery.

> *Your Zinka*

Bertie himself needed no persuasion; and as for Pino, he'd follow his crotch.

*I*t was Brocard's sincere hope that this night he might stay firmly with the text, being transported no farther than the end table for more tea or, at the farthest limits, the window of his room for a view out across the campus. He had to admit, as he picked up Judy's manuscript, that his living circumstances were very comfortable indeed. Far more pleasant than the rectory he cohabited in Bryn Mawr, with that wacky pastor lurking about. And exceedingly more agreeable than the dilapidated Monastery of San Redempto, the grim home in Rome where he had spent the better part of his priestly life. Troublesome sojourns into early modern France aside, the Mount was more than he could have hoped for. The quarters he had been provided with were spacious and clean, the campus he overlooked as elegant as it was manicured. No reason to complain; every reason to rejoice.

To make sure nothing untoward happened, he carefully followed Avertanus' instructions, lighting the candle and repeating the incantation the proscribed number of times. Then, opening the manuscript he read:

> *While Madame Guyon was making a retreat at the Abbey of Malhoue, less than ten miles outside of town she received the news that her father was gravely ill. He died before she could return. And then, only three days later, her three year old daughter Marie-Anne, the child she had doted on more than any of the others, died as well.*

How very, very sad. Despite the centuries of time that separated them, Brocard could not help but feel her loss. He too had lost his father early in life and, because of the demands of religion, been unable to be there when he most needed to be. Why is it, he thought, that those who are drawn to religious experiences, mystics and pseudo-mystics alike, all suffer great losses early in life? It was as if she stood in front of him, in his very room, inconsolable in grief. Until, that is, he realized that it was not his room at all that he was in, but hers. Once again, he inhabited her world.

Black crepe was everywhere—bunched onto the valances, draped over the furniture, swathed around her fragile form. Grief was palpable, a grief which the man who was attending Madame Guyon reflected in speech and behavior. It was hard for Brocard to identify, but there was something evil about this man with his high-handed piety and overly refined ways. He wanted so much to call out to Madame Guyon, to tell her to beware. But he could not cross into her life that completely, nor would her grief have even allowed anyone or anything to enter.

"God punishes because that is the nature of his divine justice. We must punish ourselves, must debase and humiliate ourselves, because God would have it no other way."

His words were so cold and Jansenistic, that Catholic Puritanism which was so very fashionable in the salons of Paris, among the ruling class. Madame Guyon lifted her veil and gave him the most piercing of looks, as if she longed to believe that these losses, especially that of her beloved daughter, made sense in God's plan. And then, surprising herself perhaps more than even Brocard, she began to laugh. Just the slightest giggle at first, a shocking recognition that she was still a girl, which mounted into a chortle then went over the top into a downright guffaw. "You have to," she said catching her breath, "you just have to be kidding."

With maniacally controlled anger, the Jansenist friend of her brother Jacque (which was all Brocard could make of the man's identity) went over to the door of the study in which they were meeting, and bolted the door. Then, taking out a silk handkerchief the scent of which nearly overwhelmed Brocard, he slowly walked over to Madame Guyon, whose face registered curiosity rather than fear—a miscalculation of major proportion.

"You worm," he hissed at her as he stuffed the handkerchief into her mouth and tied it tight around her neck. "You wretched piece of slime," he whispered into her ear as he threw her down onto the floor and raised her skirt. Little more was said as the faceless Jansenist mounted Madame Guyon and thrust himself into her unconscious body over and over again.

Brocard alone was heard to scream as the horror of the act unfolded before him.

11

Zinka's cell bore less of a resemblance to a monastery than to a utilitarian cubicle. In fact, the whole commune—from furniture to labyrinthine corridors to the initiates themselves—could well have sprung from the tormented mind of that greatest of Czech writers, Kafka. The Church of the Age of Doom, housed as it was in a sinister medieval pile, hovered—as did Kafka's own Castle—over villagers who knew little of its ways except that it controlled their lives. Literary as the reference might have been, it was far from consoling to Zinka as she aimlessly wandered the corridors in search of information.

It would have been premature to say that she was looking for clues. A body would be nice, of course. But really anything would be helpful, as she knew next to nothing about the commune or, for that matter, her sister the High Priestess. But where to start?

Compounding Zinka's frustration was the fact that there was no one to speak with, no one to charm and cajole—two of her major talents. However, there were endless rooms for her to slip into and nose around, so that at least her other true talent could be used. Namely, snooping.

She came across a rather charming, if somewhat bizarre, painting in an unused reading room. The upper left hand quadrant was dominated by a radiant Madonna pressing on an exposed breast; while the lower was taken up by a kneeling saint, arms extended in ecstatic prayer, eyes fixed on our Lady. Connecting these two visual poles was a stream of milk shooting out from her tit and arching, rather impressively, into the eagerly open mouth of the saint. Baroque details abounded from broken columns to swirling putti, but it was, after all, the ebullient content and affective composition that made the painting truly Baroque—not to mention its kinkiness. Although Bohemian paintings were not Zinka's area, as a trained art historian she nevertheless recognized it as a genuine Bendl, not just by the legible signature but by the assuredness of the style and technique. It was curious to have found such a surprising gem of a work outside a museum or church.

There was a quiet rustle of someone moving behind her: prey.

"Please," she said to the retreating young woman in the doorway, "you don't have to go because of me."

"I am so sorry to disturb you." She was clearly visibly shaken at being in Zinka's presence—something the zoftic Zinka had long since gotten used to. "I always disturb people, it seems. Am always making a mess of things."

"On the contrary," she said pushing out her breasts and laying on the charm, "I was looking for company. In fact, I was just saying to myself just now, 'Zinka, wouldn't it be nice to have the company of an attractive, virile girl to help me through this interminably long afternoon.'"

A diminutive piece of female meat, Zinka thought as she glided over to her—a twenty year-old's body and the mind of half as many years. Dumb and cute—the way she like them.

"My name is Zinka," she cooed, "what's yours?"

"Sophia." The name gave her a start as the association she had with it was of hidden wisdom. Still she forged on. "Poetic name, Sophia. Are you an initiate then?"

"Yes." Her voice faltered as she tried to look her in the eyes but couldn't make it past her bosom. "Aren't all of us here? Initiates, I mean."

"Of sorts, I guess. I'm really just having a look-see. You know, getting a feel for things."

"Didn't you have to sign the papers, then?"

"Sign paper I did," Zinka assured Sophia as she pressed up close to her and closed the door behind them so they would have some privacy. "I make it a point of never reading anything I sign. Far too tedious and, anyway, if it's important someone will let you know sooner or later." Sophia tried to return Zinka's smile but by now she was breaking out into a cold sweat and trembling ever so slightly. "Well, was there something I should have read then?"

"I don't think we are suppose to be talking," Sophia said so quietly that Zinka had to strain to hear. "I mean, if you're an observer and I'm an initiate, as I am, then we are definitely not supposed to be talking."

There were questions Zinka wanted to ask—about the commune's rule of silence and the secrets this was meant to keep hidden—but young miss Sophia seemed to be doing just fine left rambling by herself. A little more discomfort might just do the trick though. Purring ever so slightly, Zinka touched her right hand and eased it up, up, up until it came to rest on her breast. Then their eyes met and she saw tears in them, and awe.

"You're a virgin then?" Sophia timidly asked Zinka.

Now even though no one had ever said anything so preposterous to Zinka in her entire life, she realized that this was not the time for one of her famous guffaws. Rather, mustering all of her restraint, she kept her dignity and, difficult as it was, said nothing.

"I knew you were a virgin. Since I first saw you I knew that you were one with the Priestess Natalia, that you too were a sacred virgin." Then, without another word, she buried her face in Zinka's breasts which, given their enormous mass, had no problem accommodating her. "We have been waiting and praying for another virgin, not that having the High Priestess in our midst is not enough. But, you know, with her connection with Father Jan, her exalted position, well, I was hoping for a virgin like you."

"Yes, yes." Zinka stroked her head soothingly as she spoke, trying not to feel like chopped liver or, at best, some second string virgin. "Yes, Father Jan," she said, hoping that repeating the name might open her still more.

"With her as the founder's virgin spouse, it made sense that she would be seated on the throne when he ascended to the right hand of the Father. But that she would feed us with the milk of grace is almost too much for us to bear. For unworthy initiates like me at least."

So you need some dried up tit like me, Zinka thought. Just

28

come right out and say it. Then again, her face pressing up against Zinka's silicon stuffed tit was rather gratifying. Thank God for little blessings. Or maybe thank Natalia and her relationship with the founder of this Cult, from whom it seems she derived her authority. And considerable money, as Zinka considered the Briedl painting alone, not to mention the real estate in which it was housed. Sis had certainly cleaned up on this one.

"Such a fine painting." Sophia pulled her face out just far enough to see what Zinka was talking about and then pushing back in, mumbling, "That was Melissa's gift offering. The Priestess is very found of it as well."

"Yes, gift offering," she repeated, holding out for more.

"Not all of us have one to give, or can get one. Most of us do though because there are so many deserted churches and manses and, being the end time, well it is our duty to save them from destruction. Me, I gift offered silver candelabra and crucifixes. Everything is accepted but the paintings are valued the most – they earn more grace. And milk."

Stolen would be more to the point, Zinka thought as her investigative juices started kicking in. She longed to talk with Melissa, to find out where exactly the painting had come from. But this was not to be as it was Melissa herself whose dead body had tripped Zinka up and been hidden from sight.

12

*I*s there any place more splendid than Prague in the spring? It was the perfect setting to offset splendid architecture that, in its turn, housed the sexiest of people. One might wish that they bathed more, but really, on any scale, there was no better place to be – especially for Bertie and his testosterone driven boyfriend, Pino. Even their differences in taste could be accommodated by this generous city, which never dictates but always allures. Like, for example, their trip to St. George's Convent, that lovely museum housed in Prague Castle.

Defrocked priest that he was, Bertie could never get enough

of religious places. So up the hill they trudged so that Bertie could spend time with one of his favorite paintings, the Johann-Adalbert Angermayer's *Still Life with Watch*. This vanity painting, which he had known in reproduction for years, seemed to have been painted for him alone, especially now that he was seeing time's ravages on his forty year old body — telltale lines around the eyes and mouth and that dryness of skin which spoke of age. For Pino, who would go to his grave without an aesthetic experience, this stroll through palatial rooms was a splendid opportunity to show off his ass. As was the stroll they later took under the soaring chancel of St. Vitus Cathedral. Pino, you see, had decided on sporting a pair of worn jeans with the back pocket strategically ripped off and torn so that a good amount of fleshy rump greeted his many admirers. Man and woman, straight and gay all deeply appreciated what they saw; and seasoned hustler that he was, Pino basked in their admiration. He just knew that many of them were regulars to his paid web site, two years old now, which followed his routine, from shit to slumber, daily. The fact that fewer and fewer people were logging on these days in no way disillusioned him, his ego being far too grand for that.

Nor was Bertie put out by the hours Pino spent cruising the cafes and alleys around the Old Town Square. After all there were plaques to read, facades to study and, on the stroke of every quarter of an hour, that wonderful mechanical clock to watch. Besides which, Bertie felt flattered that everyone lusted after his boyfriend, never once, self-effacing as he was, worthy of being cruised himself. Not that he was that bad, little Bertie. But you had to admit that he was a plain looking chap whose better days were in the past.

All of this is to say that they were an inseparable couple, ideally suited one to the other. Bertie loved Pino; and Pino loved Pino too, and truly needed someone like Bertie who understood this deep and abiding passion.

After two blissful days in Prague they boarded the train for the Bohemian countryside to put their asses at the service of their friend Zinka. It was, however, another appendage of Pino's that Zinka would most need.

Avertanus, my dear friend,

Would that we could sit down together as in happier times and talk over all that is happening. I cannot help but feel that our having to resort to email, efficient though it might be, diminishes the quality of our communication. This having been said, I am still enormously grateful that we at least have this means, as I see myself in increased need of your advice and support.

My most recent sojourns with Madame Guyon have been truly harrowing. In the first, you will excuse my being indelicate but it must be said, I witnessed her being brutally raped by a self-righteous and nameless Jansenist, who left as his calling card, his seed implanted in her womb. My second and most recent entry into her life, was the equally unsettling scene of her giving birth to a strapping creature that she called Jeanne-Marie even before the blood was washed off. In both instances this admirable woman said nothing, but the pain etched on her face was so intense that it brought tears to my eyes.

It seems from Judy's paper that at least one historian, the great Louis Cognet (one of the sources for spirituality of the period), suspected that this last offspring might have been a child of rape. This is how Judy McCabe puts it:

As for the birth, making no direct connection with this meeting with the Jansenist with whom she ardently discussed matters of faith, Cognet very interestingly says that "with great internal struggle and a particularly painful labour," Madame Guyon gave birth to a child that she named Jeanne-Marie after herself, on March 21, 1676.

How I long to tell Judy that it was in fact true. Like Artemesia Gentilleschi — that wondrous Renaissance artist, under-appreciated to our time — and other women on strength in times past, a man who resented her power and wisdom indeed assaulted Madame Guyon. How this would strengthen Judy's paper and her entire case, as it is becoming increasingly clear that her retrieval of Guyon is a thoroughly sympathetic one. But what would she footnote? My occult time-travel? How credible would that be after all to the academy? So you see my dilemma, my dear friend. What I must do is keep silent in the face of rape, injustice and indeed historical inaccuracy which removes this poor soul from the realm of sympathy into that of privileged piety.

I am becoming increasingly reluctant to go back into Madame Guyon's time, for fear of what I might see, indeed might experience as I am no passive voyeur. Just before writing you I opened to my bookmark and read this sentence:

Exactly four months later to the day, after a long illness, her husband dies. She was a twenty-eight-year-old wealthy widow.

Given the horrors that had transpired it might not have been so bad to have been by her side at the end of this love-less arranged marriage. It seemed just and right that Madame was now as rich in money as she most assuredly was in suffering.

> *Your friend always,*

> *Brocard*

14

*N*o one realized how difficult it was. Being Zinka's life companion was something akin to riding out a tornado. Where in the vortex Camille found herself at any given moment was impossible to say. But love her she did; and stand by her she would, although many would think her foolish.

When others looked at Camille they saw a smart Parisian lady of a certain age who was always impeccably turned out, right down to her signature Hermes scarf and open-toed high heels. What she hadn't earned as a respected antiquarian, she had inherited from her haute bourgeois parents. This included a tiny but tasteful apartment on Avenue Foch in the seizième arrondissement and a collection of jewelry that spoke of quiet elegance.

During those rare moments when Camille was forced to regard herself, however, something quite different was seen. She saw a woman riddled by self-doubt and fear; a woman who wanted nothing more than to lose herself in another woman, because men were as repugnant to her as a bloody steak to a vegetarian. She saw a woman who was aging with frightening rapidity; a woman whose last chance both at emotional and sexual happiness was this larger than life transsexual, without whom she simply could not live.

So it was that Camille found herself driving along the Seine towards that most monstrous of Grand Projects, the Bibliothèque Nationale, to do research for and to validate her existence in service to her Zinka. It was a perfect day for reflection: an oppressive sky, penetrating dampness, all so unremitting gray — so very Parisian. Nothing whatsoever to detract her from replaying in her mind the telephone conversation she had with her girlfriend, the love of her life, earlier that morning.

"My tight little cabbage, do you miss your Zinka? What is that, a little moan? For Zinka it's a long plaintive moan or nothing. That's better."

"Have you managed to locate your sister."

"Natalia, oh my dear, Natalia. What tits that girl has and, you wouldn't believe it, she is suckling the world. With milk, my randy little pumpkin, do you hear me? Milk. And they call her a virgin."

"She's a lactating virgin, your sister? How very fine."

"I knew you would get off on that, my twisted little pretzel. But here is what I need from you. Get out your pencil and take this down."

Then Zinka made a list of what she wanted Camille to research, from the Bohemian Baroque to the lactating virgin trope to the Interpol List of Art and precious objects stolen from Balkan Churches. Were Camille anything less of a researcher and willing slave she would surely have balked at this request. As it was, she delighted in the fact that she could be of help.

In fact, Camille was beside herself that Zinka needed her assistance. Her greatest fear when she had heard that Zinka was going in search of her roots was that long-lost relatives would pop out of the woodwork — obviating any emotional need Zinka might have for her. The whole thought of family—something she lived happily without—quite truthfully terrified Camille as it might lay claim to parts of a girlfriend that she had hoped was hers and hers alone. Now, at least, there was work that Camille might do not only to prove her worth but also to lay some claim to this new part of Zinka's life.

Much of what Zinka had said that morning was not fully clear, to either Camille or Zinka it might be said. She could not get over the way in which her little sister Natalia had changed. Not just in bust size but in every way. She had been so shy, so withdrawn and fragile—so unlike the zaftig earth mother demanding the worship of a community of tortured followers. But she had always liked fine things, that Natalia, and she seemed to have inherited the wealth to secure them, which added to her admitted allure.

As Camille paid the taxi and made her way into the Biblioteque, she had the unsettling feeling that Zinka was becoming attracted to her own sister. At the very least, fascinated— a rivalry Camille could do without.

15

A mustiness clung to everything in the room—part mildew, part human sweat—but neither Madame Guyon nor her traveling companion were even remotely fazed by it. They were so caught up in prayer that even the noise in the tavern below in no way troubled them. Their eyes closed and their hands resting folded in their laps, she on the corner of the bed, he in the straight back chair near the door, they were as separate from each other as two bodies could be. Yet Brocard knew, as one who himself had experienced such prayer, as deeply connected as two souls are capable.

His name was Père Lacombe, a Barnabite priest who she had met through one of her several half-brothers. And with whom she had struck up an instant rapport as both of them were graced, that was the only word for it, with the same mystical experiences. They both knew that this set them apart from others whose faith was on a lower level. Guyon spoke with Lacombe and they understood each other, as in the words they now muttered.

"The Ground burns within me, its heat overwhelming."

"Light, blinding light pours out from me."

At these last words, Madame opened her eyes ever so slightly to see if the light was pouring out from him. But it was the heat, the flame burning within her which was of greater concern and, in an attempt to deal with it, she let the shawl drop from her shoulders and unlaced her bodice.

"Come," she muttered to some unseen force, "come into me now."

Just then there was a rap on the door and a barmaid came in with two plates of mutton. She smiled slightly at the scene, the woman on the bed, the man near her covered in sweat, something she was quite used to seeing usually, but shocking even to her. This lady, after all, was no ordinary guest but a woman of rank and property; and, this man was, after all, a priest. Everyone knew that they were going to speak about prayer and God and things like that at the local church that night. It was all right for a barmaid to behave like this but everyone of reason had to draw the line at this.

Brocard could see, however, that neither Lacombe nor Madame were concerned about what others thought. It was as if they were unfettered by petty moral codes, free to live in the Spirit that coursed within them.

If there was anything that disturbed Père Lacombe, it was the overwhelming presence, the almost awesome person, of this mystical woman, for whom he would have sacrificed everything. In fact, there was not much more that he could give up for her: his community had disowned him because of what they perceived as scandalous behavior. His Provincial had ordered him to desist from traveling around the Savoy and South Eastern France, areas where Protestantism was rife and Catholic decorum had to be held to the highest standards, with this wealthy widow, which, of course, he could not do. Madame Guyon had assured him that it was God's will and hers that he accompanied her throughout France to give witness to the transforming power of the Prayer of Quiet. Following her indefatigable lead, he saw how important it was that all Catholics stop piling devotion on top of devotion. All that was necessary was to still themselves and listen to the voice within; the godhead erupting in their very ground.

Sex never consciously entered into their thinking but it surely was there. For Guyon all physicality died on the floor of the library where she had been pinned down and torn open. For Lacombe, a man who had never known woman or man in the remotest of biblical senses, the smell of this creature, her dilated eyes in prayer, her bosoms spilling out, confusion rained—a confusion that was quite literally to drive him mad.

Brocard heard a great racket in the hallway and moved over to the window to get out of the way. There was no polite knock as the door swung open and four officers stormed into the room. Lacombe was seized as he lunged towards Madame to protect her, but she needed no protection as she was shielded by God's power. She knew that she would be taken to the Visitation Nuns on the Faubourg St. Augustin in Paris where she was to be 'put under supervision'. This was the fate that she was often threatened with and she knew that the time had finally come. Lacombe, unfortunately, having neither money nor power, was not to be so favorably treated.

Brocard was happy to be returned to his room at the Court, to his cooling pot of tea and uncomplicated life. How amazing that any human being would fall so completely under the sway of another. Even if they claimed to be the spokesperson of God. Extinguishing the candle and turning up the lights so he was sure he would not relapse into the seventeenth century, Brocard thumbed through Judy's paper to see what had happened to poor Père Lacombe. His fate, it seemed, was worse than he had imagined.

Father Lacombe was imprisoned, first in the Bastille then later in the castle at Lourdes where he went crazy and took his own life.

16

*D*reary was an understatement. Apocalyptically

appalling, suicidally sinister were more accurate. Yet all words would have been inadequate to convey the unremitting grimness of the Castle Church of the Age of Doom, temporary home of Zinka and demesne of her sister the Priestess Natalia.

It was not just the windowless gray pile of stone that was so off-putting, but the site of the Castle itself. Pressed up against a vertiginous pile of mud and rocks, it seemed more like aged detritus than historic architecture. In happier times, there were no doubt trees and flowering bushes crowning it; now, deforested by villagers too lazy to walk into the forest for wood, it was little more than a slag-heap. Even a castle of worth, which this had never been, would be unwelcoming in such a setting.

Still, they were called to help Zinka and, to this end, both Bertie and Pino girded their loins and set about their task — quicker than they imagined.

"Pstt!" Subtle, Zinka never was, especially when she was trying to be. "Over here!"

Pino and Bertie ran over to the door that Zinka was not too successfully hiding behind, air-kissed her rapidly in greeting.

"We should not be seen talking," she went on, "after all you are newly arrived initiates and as for me," looking coy and cool, "I'm a virgin."

"Really my darling, get a grip on things."

"I'll explain later Bertie my precious defrocked cleric. Right now, there's work to be done."

Never being one for repartee, Pino was trying valiantly to adjust his tunic, realizing all the while that it highlighted his cock in the most flattering of ways. Light fabric pulsated around his most admirable feature.

"Now that, my dear large Pino," she said stroking it shamelessly, "is exactly what the doctor ordered."

Realizing that it would be insensitive for a boyfriend not to react in some way — even though Pino was nothing short of public property — Bertie coughed, as if wanting to say something.

"Calm down, Bertie, it's not for me. It's for the sake of truth and justice. Or, at the very least, finding out where they hid the bodies."

"Bodies?" It was the two of them that spoke this time, since all they had heard about was one disappearing corpse.

"Just last night. This time at least I saw a dead body being dragged down the hallway. Another middle-aged woman — but who exactly, I don't know. Nor have I any idea how she died — or was killed. Nothing except the identity of the disposer, if that's even a word. Her name is Sophia, a squat looking girl with a predilection for big breasted women."

"Sounds like more your line of work than mine," Pino said disparagingly. There was nothing he liked less than being outshone.

"Even though she has this maternal longing which, between us, gets very old very quickly, it seems to me, my dear Pino, that she's your 'man.' Penetrate the fortress, my happy stud. And her as well, just so long as you use a condom. Come closer and I'll tell you where to find her, how to lure her and, most importantly, what I need to know."

17

*C*amille was that rarest of women, solid as a brick and constant as the pole star. Which to her thinking, meant that she was a total bore. Granted she engendered trust, but was that enough to keep Zinka by her side? This was the question without an answer that she had to live with, being constitutionally incapable of spontaneity and sparkle. So she did the research Zinka required of her, paid the bills and did the chores, hoping against hope that the sum total of these mundane tasks would equal an ounce of *je ne sais quoi*.

The Bibliothèque Nationale was every bit as helpful as it was ugly. Within the space of an hour Camille had printed out several articles on the Bohemian Baroque, especially Briedl. The Lactating Virgin image was indeed a minor yet significant trope of the period. What was harder to find, however, were Interpol records for stolen liturgical art and objects from that region of Central Europe. She found one significant memo that indicated that a considerable amount of art could well be plundered. Many churches and religious houses had gone to ruin during the fifty years of communist occupation; and, compounding the problem, accurate inventory of these items was never kept as much was hidden or, worse still, forgotten. In other words, as Zinka might say, it was a candy store just waiting to be eaten.

Having time to kill, Camille decided to stroll along the Seine until she was run out of energy and then find a taxi rank. She knew that she couldn't make it all the way back to Avenue Foch with her heels; still, the exercise would do her good.

What saddened her even more than the grayness of the day and the fog that hung close to the banks of the river, was the fact that no one noticed her. Not one furtive glance, not one glint of lust, not even a perfunctory nod. Nothing. It was as if she were invisible. Worse still: undesirable — something a woman of a certain age loathes to be reminded of.

As she was approaching the Rue Napoleon near the entrance to the *Ecole des Beaux Arts*, an elegantly dressed obese man stopped in his tracks to greet her. Better than nothing, she thought, then saw that it was Emile Rothenberg, the former director of the Louvre to whom Zinka had been so rude.

"Madame Blanchierderie, how pleasant to see you."

"*Docteur* Rothenberg, *enchantée*."

"I had no idea you were still in Paris, convinced as I was that you had succumbed to the charms of Rome."

"Very much in Paris, *Docteur*. Professoressa Pavlik," present circumstances dictated she refer to Zinka in the most exalted of manners, "Professoressa Zinka Pavlik, you will remember, and I are pleasantly ensconced and in no way tempted to return to Rome, at least for the time being."

Sweat poured out from under Emile's Hamburg, which he doused with a fine linen handkerchief and his breath was excruciatingly labored. Please God, Camille thought, let him expire after I've gone. Or at least let him collapse into the nearest café chairs so he doesn't tumble onto the Rue Napoleon and make a spectacle of the two of us.

The chair it was. And rather than have Camille flutter about like a vulture, he signaled for her to take the chair next to him. Without asking her, he huffed "Du thé" to the nearest garçon and, regaining some composure, simply said, "beastly heat."

"I have been doing some research for the Professoressa, to help her with her latest investigation." Not being sure what to say—it must be appalling to be so obese, how profusely you sweat—Camille thought it best to be professional. "She's in the Czech countryside at the moment, scouting out stolen Bohemian Baroque paintings. Which, as I recall," Camille added trying to be civil, "is one of your areas of expertise."

"Such a clever woman your Professoressa." Emile leaned sideways and slightly forward to avoid the sun, a careening move that Camille found quite unsettling. "So remarkably unlike any other art historian I have ever encountered, I can assure you." Then, seeing that Camille was slightly offended, quickly added, "would that there were more academics who took an active interest in the solving of such mysteries."

"Granted her techniques are rather different, unique even. Still one must admit that this obsession of hers to identify and retrieve stolen arts, is well founded." Dr. Rothenberg was feeling just a bit uncomfortable about the way in which the conversation was going but decided this was nothing that a little pastry could not remedy.

As the tea was brought to the table and poured into their cups, Emile ruminated as only a man of his girth could do, on the word 'obsession.' Finally pronouncing both the tea and this word itself, splendid. Then settling back into the sturdy rattan chair in which he was so comfortably ensconced, he began to discourse on the nature of obsession.

"It is, one might say, the ground and origin of all that is good and bad in humanity—this obsession. And women, if you will excuse my gender specific reference, women are the supreme masters of it. They control obsession, their own and the obsession they engender and nourish in others, with such sublimity that it must be in their very nature."

Camille was not sure where this was going, nor, for that matter, how comfortable she was with such sexist talk. Still, at the risk of getting the pedant's blood pressure up, she held her tongue. There was, after all, a possibility that he has something to say.

"Ronald Knox, the Anglican preacher who wrote so eloquently about enthusiasm, as he called it, saw it as the basis for all mystical experience—both real and delusional. Characters such as the remarkable Madame Guyon of our Golden Age were marked by a single-mindedness that would brook no dissent. Her obsessive behavior changed all in her path, for good or bad. Some freed themselves from the constraints of organized religion; others, well, others went clearly mad, didn't they? And that is the nature of obsession. It has the ability to move us into higher realms or condemn us to a living hell."

How much should Camille reveal about Zinka's current project? Was there any danger in sharing it, at least globally, with this aging aesthete who had played a part in both the Poussin and the Caravaggio mysteries? No danger, Camille thought, none at all.

"The Baroque paintings and liturgical objects which I was researching for Zinka are housed in a New Age Commune that fits perfectly into your description of obsession." Content to sit back and listen, Emile Rothenberg played the student to Camille, eager to hear all that she had to tell him. "The guru, if you will, is a charismatic young woman whose vision of impending world doom seems to have enthralled both men and women. Both straight and gay, it is interesting to note, are mesmerized by her." Lowering her voice more for effect than for privacy, Camille confided "the Professoressa called me last night to say that she had enlisted the help of a Roman hustler. It seems that he had already identified one of the key initiates of the community and was about to lure her into telling him what he knows. We both feel, the Professoressa and I, as if he must know something about where all of the art has come from. Interpol suggests churches and monasteries in Bohemia are being plundered but has no specific information." Then, leaning forward for added impact, Camille added. "there are two bodies as well, quite dead."

One of the fortunate aspects of morbid obesity is that emotions lie undetected in rolls of fat. Of course, Emil Rothenberg's pulse raced at this news, but nothing about him showed it. All that was clear was that, on some level, he had to involve himself with the activity in Bohemia. Professionally, and yes, personally, involve himself, because so very much was at stake.

Stirring his tea a bit too forcefully, he proclaimed to Camille, in the most professorial of tone, "The obsession, my good Madame Blanchierderie, of which I speak, extends to the admirable Professoressa Zinka. Long may her lust for justice continue."

18

"*C*areful, careful." The problem with girls is that they never get to practice blowing and when they are finally given the chance, they attack a cock rather than woo it. "Just slow down," Pino ordered reassuringly, "it's not going anywhere—and it's all yours."

Tears were forming in Sophia's eyes as she looked up at Pino's godlike body. It was hard to tell exactly what these tears signified: relief at having her fantasy made real? Joy of knowing that there was a man who understood her obsession? Or perhaps just asphyxiation caused by the blockage of her windpipes? Did it really matter anyway?

"Lick it, that's right, lick it slowly." Sophia was in the zone, the slave zone. Having driven so many there, Pino could recognize it well and knew that now he could ask anything and it would not, indeed it could not be denied him.

"These paintings," Pino said looking around the room, remarkably detached from the woman who was sucking him off, "they're stolen, right?"

Sophia mumbled something. "Don't speak with your mouth full. Just grunt once for yes and two times for no." Then trying again, "They're stolen, right?" To which Sophia grunted yes.

"Are there more paintings like these around?" Another single grunt. "Any more of these tit feeding ones?" Grunt. "She likes milking tits this Natalia, doesn't she?" Grunt.

"Now tell me about the dead bodies." For the briefest of moments Pino could feel the tongue stop working, then, knowing there was no way that she could stop, the saliva kept dripping. "Did you dispose of the bodies?"

Sophia looked up at him helplessly. There were things she couldn't say. But Pino knew how to handle that. Taking her head between his hands, he thrust himself deep into Sophia's throat and held it there, gagging her into delirium.

"Did you get rid of the bodies or didn't you?" A soft but discernible grunt as Pino pushed Sophia down onto the floor and stood, exposed, over her.

"Who steals the art?" He asked as he pushed her away.

"Initiates."

"Did the two bodies steal art?"

"Offered them," Sophia said beseechingly. But Pino needed answers, not gratification, which he could get anytime he wanted. "So they gave them to this Church, alright. Then why were they killed?"

"Not killed." She sobbed. "They took their own lives."

"Why did they kill themselves?"

"The promise. The reward."

Here Pino leaned back against the wall and offered himself to Sophia as a reward. Her face was bloated and pupils as dilated as someone possessed, but God help her, she was a happy girl. There was one final question he had to ask.

"What could lead anyone to rob and then to kill themselves?"

"Obsessed." Sophia shriveled up on the floor as Pino jerked off over her.

As his shot arched out into the air, Pino calmly concurred. "Tell me about it."

*B*rocard was not easily impressed. Between meetings with cardinals and archbishops and even, on occasion, a sighting of the Holy Father himself, he had seen his fair share of important personages. However, here he was in the presence of one of the most influential of Christian theologians, a man whom many considered a saint—not to mention someone who had been dead for almost three hundred years.

It is safe to say that he had expected Fénelon to be more impressive in real life—at the very least, to have a pious paunch or a furrowed brow. But in fact the great man was a fresh-faced thirty-seven year old cleric, thin as a rail and, although he carried himself well, not overly distinguished in bearing. What Brocard had to assume was that Fénelon, who by this age was a friend of luminaries such as Bérulle—and a distinguished doctor of spirituality in his own right—was at the height of his intellectual powers. What shocked him was that Madame Guyon, seated at a writing desk, saw herself as every bit his match.

"The Duchess of Béthune said that you have been writing spiritual works," Fénelon said in the calmest of tones.

"They come to me," the young widow replied, in the most assured of tones. "From my heart, it seems, where they originate—from, if you will, the ground of being."

"Study, research, intellectual prowess," he continued, "these mean nothing to you?"

"Nothing at all." There was no disrespect in what she had said only a need to be direct and honest. "The heart, my dear Father, is all. The mind only breeds confusion."

A ray of light, brilliant as the sun itself, broke through the passing clouds and streamed into the convent chamber where they were meeting. Shielding his eye from its glare, Fénelon moved nearer to the web of darkness in which she was seated. Madame Guyon registered how close he was moving to her, with palpable anticipation.

"Does it not bother you to be confined to the Visitation

sisters?"

"I am indifferent to it, as I am to all things of this earth." Then, as she realized that he was a pragmatic man who needed practical answers, she added, "besides, father, they treat me well. They supply me with all of the paper and ink I could ever need, food and all of the privacy one could hope for in order to fall totally under the sway of God."

"May I see what it is you are writing?" He had moved over to her desk by now and, slight as he was, towered over her like a shade tree. She placed her hand on his as he went to pick up the page she had been writing; caught his eyes with hers, then gently placed a sheaf of loose pages into his hand. "These are finished, ready for you to read."

Fénelon picked up the document entitled *Le Moyen Court; L'Explication du Cantique des Cantiques*, turned rapidly through it, page after page, in disbelief.

"Not a single correction; not a misplaced word. Surely this is a fine copy?"

"The effusions of my heart appear and are set down whole and perfect."

Brocard, having had humility drummed into him from an early age, was astounded at this young woman's self-assurance — her arrogance in fact. The reality, as he saw it, indeed as it surely was, was that Madame Guyon was a hopelessly uneducated woman; and that Fénelon, in contrast, was one of the most educated men of his time. What insanity, what delusion or what inspiration permitted her to so diminish this man?

For more than an hour the young theologian sat beside the widow and read the text that she had written. Occasionally he spoke out loud some words which caught his attention, and which to Brocard seemed like dross: saintly indifference, abandonment.

Finally, taking her hand and looking deep into her eyes, he admitted his problem was a "passion for reason." Why, Brocard thought, must passion rear its ugly head?

*F*or those of us not blessed with the facility to travel through time, cyberspace offers a pleasant alternative. Undoubtedly Avertanus was somewhat jealous of the experiences Brocard was having. But he still felt graced and privileged to live in a world where communication was not hindered by space or time—to inhabit a world where friends in rural Bohemia and Pennsylvania could speed their thoughts to him in Holland. And where he, in the comfort of his cell, could consider and rapidly respond to them.

Carissimo Avertanus, my dearest sage,

So much is happening so quickly that I don't know where to begin. Pino, who you might remember as the hustler for whom Father Bertie left your religious order, has been most helpful in helping me penetrate the mysteries of the Age of Doom. Between us, I think he's penetrating a bit more than he needs to. But once a whore always a whore, as my mother told me. It seems that there is a bundle of stolen art in this godforsaken castle. How much it is impossible to tell as dear Camille has found almost no Interpol records for pilfered Bohemian art. Which means that all of this stuff, a series of wondrous Baroque lactating virgins most especially, might not be technically stolen at all.

Another snag that has come up concerns these dead bodies, two to date, which I have been stumbling across. According to Pino's penetrated source—who, it does seem has a deep throat, but let's not go there—they took their own lives. Which means that these are not murders at all, but technically suicides.

In the midst of it all is beautiful Natalia, my poor unsuspecting baby sister, who still has no idea that her brother—transformed into the glorious me—has returned. The Return of Ulysses to his Homeland, you might say, disguised as I am so that I can take revenge on all of those who would exploit my Penelope. Needless to say, this is a strained metaphor, but you, my wise old scholar, can untangle it for me. My point being, of course, that Natalia is surely being thoroughly used in this situation. How I long to tell her of the intrigues swirling around her before she becomes hopelessly entangled in them. If, that is, my dearest Avertanus, things have not already spiralled out of control. As patiently as I am able, I await your kind feedback.

Kisses. Zinka

Avertanus allowed some time for Zinka's world to invade his own. How strange that bleak commune must be, housed as it is in a decrepit castle pressed up against a forlorn hillside. And how ill advised it would be for him to offer advice at such a distance and with such scattered impressions of what was happening. He had serious doubts about the innocence of the High Priestess Natalia, baby sister or not. But how could he tell Zinka?

Dear Professoressa Zinka,

You are so kind to look on me as wise. I do so hate to disillusion you, but, alas, I must. About bodies — be they suicide or butchered — and stolen art, I know so very little. The Lactating Virgin Trope, however, I am quite familiar with as it runs deep in the mystical tradition. St. Bernard of Clairvaux was among the first to develop it. He goes so far as to suckle the breast of God himself, which is an image worth pondering. The virgin's milk is ostensibly grace; but one cannot remove the possibility of a certain prurient interest on the part of both saints and sinners throughout the centuries. As for your sister Natalia, no doubt you are right about her naïveté, still, I caution you on jumping to any conclusions. Things might not be as they seem. The situation that you find yourself in seems Byzantine to the extreme.

Your friend,

Father Avertanus

The second email that greeted him came from his dear friend Brocard, who, it seemed, was finally coming around. In fact, his enthusiasm was downright infectious.

Father Avertanus, my advisor and friend,

You'll notice that I refer to you as 'father' because I truly appreciate the way in which you have helped me. You are truly, as Paul said of himself, a Father in Service. I refer, in case you had any doubts, to the way in which you have cajoled and recommended, advised and guided me in bitemporation – that remarkable facility of simultaneously being both in this time and some historic past. What had originally seemed the most wrenching of experiences has become an unadulterated grace.

Avertanus, I have met Cardinal Fénelon. Well, not yet a Cardinal – or anything like that wizened, crease lined visage so familiar to us from spirituality texts. No, the Fénelon I was privileged to see was young and vital and so very much caught up in the experience of God that it was not difficult to see how he would have gotten himself in trouble with the Church. I also, for the first time, understood the critical role Madame Guyon played in his struggle. How beneficial she was in helping him break loose the bonds of over-intellectualization and seeing faith as primarily a matter of the heart. His struggle might well be mine. Could it be that the young widow might be reaching out to me as well?

Enthusiasm, Avertanus knew, was a two-edged sword. He prayed that Brocard, like Fénelon before him, was not losing his critical faculties. He prayed it was not too late.

21

*P*rague was more to her liking than Vienna. Far more. Vienna, after all, is the most imperial and masculine of the world's capitals, with its maniacal city-planning and grand ceremonial parade route. Prague, on the other hand, is feminine in its organic whole, respecting diversity of architecture, the gentle roll of the land and flow of the river. Vienna commanded; Prague allured. And Camille, for one, fell under its spell.

Needless to say, given the option of applying for admission into the Church of the Age of Doom, Camille chose the Prague office rather than the main one in Vienna. A few days there would give her the opportunity to get used to the sounds and smells of the Czech Republic—a region she had not visited since the bloodless split with its poor relative, Slovakia. Why, after all, would they have fought to keep hold of the problem? Letting it peacefully go was a stroke of good fortune.

Prosperity was everywhere, from her renovated hotel near the Charles Bridge to the neatly folded napkins at the café on the Old Town Square in which she was seated. She had taken the Church of the Age of Doom application forms with her, saying that she needed time to consider this significant move in her life. In reality, Camille was determined to go behind the wall, to be with her girlfriend Zinka. What she did want to know though was what were the perimeters of her behavior, what was expected of her while there so that her presence would not raise undue alarm so as to put Zinka's mission in jeopardy. It was bad enough she was planning to arrive unannounced. The thought of this reunion with the love of her life backfiring into resentment was too horrid for words.

When the frothy cold beer arrived—Prague being inconceivable without beer, Camille started to read through a description of the lifestyle she was about to embark on:

"These bodies of ours," the top of the form announced, "are mere shells which are to be used and discarded. They are as nothing, in a world of nothingness."

Such bleakness did not sit well with Camille. In Paris, perhaps, where all is gray—but not here, in a city of pastel buildings, under a cloudless sky. Besides, she thought as she watched groups of bra-less girls scurry past her, their perky young tits bouncing away, how could anyone call boobs like that nothing? She blushed to think that her mind could be so filthy. Then, taking a hearty gulp of beer, reconsidered—what the hell.

"Are you willing to abandon any signs of outward worth by wearing a simple white tunic?" "Are you willing to move slowly, never running or hastening, always keeping to a steady rhythm?" "Are you willing to keep custody of the eyes?" (Here there was an explanation of this spiritual technique—never raising your eyes from above the level of someone's knees, never looking at anyone except the High Priestess herself). "Are you willing to speak only when spoken to? To do anything only when instructed by an Adept?" (Here an explanation was given of the position of an Adept, one of the few chosen to convey the inspired orders of the High Priestess).

To say that she was embarking on a life of consummate boredom was an understatement. Nevertheless, even though Camille read and signed her agreement to the statement that she would not seek out or converse with any other initiate, she knew that there would be an opportunity for her to be with her Zinka. She knew that somewhere in that grim, forbidding castle, they would be able to snatch a moment together. And that they would have unbridled sex, because sex was the very air that Zinka breathed.

Undaunted by the rules and galvanized by the challenge, Camille Blanchierderie, librarian and lover, polished off her beer and set off for the Castle of the Age of Doom.

22

*T*here would be no sting to this death. The High Priestess had assured him. Even without her personal solicitation, he had no doubt that the transition would be painless and beneficial on every level. Earthly existence—his in particular it is safe to say—was a senseless affair after all. A series of dashed dreams and meaningless suffering - capricious at best, masochistic, if one was to accept it fully, at base. This hard-won knowledge had led him to the decisive act he was to take—a suicide that was in fact a prelude to life.

Unfortunately, as is often the case when we make fixed plans for just about anything, the weather was not cooperating. A mild, cloudy day, perhaps a hint of fog would have been superb for a suicide. Not, however, the driving rain which was not only making the air pestilent, but also eroding the hill behind so that mud was steadily and inexorably seeping into his cell. Earlier in the morning a great glob of it had pushed its way through the partially opened window through which, ironically, he had hoped to get some fresh air. Now, of course, it was too late to close it, as he had neither a shovel nor bricks to dam it up. Anyway, shortly he would be in another dimension, joyously waiting the Priestess and her ever-gracious breast, protected from the coming apocalypse.

He recalled as he pressed the wrinkles out of his bed sheets, how happy he had made Natalia (he called her this in his heart, though never, of course, out loud) when he brought her the first Briedl painting. No one would miss it, he knew, as there hadn't been a priest in the rectory for more than twenty years. The few parishioners who still came to St. Joachim's were happy to see a few sacred vessels on the altar. Doubtless, they all thought the communists had plundered anything of value fifty years before. But Jan knew better. In fact, he had found out during his time at the Church of the Age of Doom that there were many Jan's, anonymous men and women in villages throughout Central Europe, who kept the secret. Their hope was that the faith would be restored and that these objects would be returned to their rightful place in worship. But no one told them about the uncertainty and corruption that 'democracy', as some called it, would bring. No one prepared them for the rampant secularism, the godlessness that they saw all around.

The High Priestess spoke clear words that they could understand. She confirmed their worse fears, explained how important they were to the new order. In her, Jan and many others found certainty and affirmation. Such a little price to pay, taking the art and once sacred objects from places of hiding so as to honor the one who would make all things right. And what an extraordinary reward awaited those who made it through the rigorous year of initiation: the promise of a painless transition to eternal transformation.

The poison he had taken only minutes before was beginning to take effect. Jan lay down calmly on his bed and closed his eyes, trying to block out any lingering doubts. Then a wrenching pain seized him and Jan's body flailed about and seized up in the most horrid of manner. Disbelief cried out from his every pour. But it was drowned out by the incessant rain and by the groaning of mud sliding into his room.

*I*t was not long before Madame Guyon was introduced, through her new acquaintance Father Fénelon, into the pious court circle presided over by Madame de Maintenon. This most fascinating of creatures started life as a penniless yet noble woman, who, through a series of strange turns became a fast friend of Queen Marie-Thérèse, the eldest Spanish infanta, and wife of Louis XIV by arranged marriage. Marie-Thérèse purportedly died in her arms. Some time later Madame de Maintenon became Louis XIV's wife, never given the title of queen. St. Cyr was her college for noble but penniless girls, as she had been. By all accounts, she was a born teacher. After the death of Louis XIV, she went into pious seclusion at St. Cyr. Peter the Great of Russia was one of the few dignitaries to ever get an audience with her. Everyone else she declined.

The privilege Brocard felt at being in the presence of the mysterious wife of the king—at her famed College of St. Cyr no less—was indescribable. Like all religious of his generation, Brocard had read of the way in which Madame de Maintenon had stood up to Jansenism. Of her personal piety and distance from the corruption of her husband's court at Versailles. She was, by all accounts, a living saint. The excitement Brocard experienced being with Fénelon was intensified into awe by this most recent apparition.

"Be so kind as to escort Madame Guyon into the salon." Brocard positioned himself in the back of the classroom, so that he had an unobstructed view of everything. It would have been gratifying to see such order and cleanliness in any century, but nothing short of a miracle in seventeenth century France. There was not a trace of unwashed private body parts or foul breath. What smells there were came from soap and starch, together with the faintest hint of fields of lavender wafting through the windows.

Once again, Brocard was impressed by the consummate composure of the young and beautiful Madame Guyon as she made a profound curtsy to Madame de Maintenon, then took a seat in the straight-backed chair which had been set out for her facing the class of girls.

"Our dear friend Pere Fénelon, tutor to his highness's grandson the Duke of Burgudy, has spoken kindly of you, as a woman of deep faith. The ladies of our seminary, committed as they are to growing in their relationship to the Lord, would surely benefit from a lesson in the prayer of quietude, which we hear you practise."

"It is not I who speak, most gracious Madame, but the very ground of my being which is in God." Then, casting a penetrating glance about the room, focusing in turn on each of the ten young women assembled for this session, she instructed them to close their eyes and listen. Except for the faintest call of a sparrow, nothing at all was to be heard in the room. And, since Madame Guyon's face radiated an inner peace and muted rapture, Brocard wondered if he too shouldn't close his eyes and listen, as he might well be missing something. But he was so intent on seeing everything—of being privy to this historic moment—his eyes remained unblinkingly open. Ready for anything.

"The fire within is all there is," she spoke quietly, her voice barely a murmur, then plunged into the deepest of silences. It was safe to say that the young ladies of St. Cyr were even more impressed at Madame Guyon's display of piety than Brocard himself was. After all, silent meditation was an integral part of his prayer life, whereas for a typical believer of that period, prayer meant words and ceremony. He could see them glancing at each other in disbelief. Could it be that commerce with God was not the private reserve of formulaic prayer? Might it even be that this woman was as connected to the Lord as many puffed up male clerics who paraded through St. Cyr? If so, what would this mean for them, as women of faith—and for their future in the church?

As Madame Guyon's bosoms expanded and contracted in hypnotic rhythm, her face flushed and shone, as if irradiated from within. Brocard knew well that she was experiencing one of her 'spiritual infusions,' but had no idea where it might lead her.

In slow and measured tones the young mystic began to speak about the persecuted Father Lacombe, the noble soul who had given his very life for the truth of quiet prayer. How proud she was, how proud God was of his faithfulness. Then, with words that bordered on blasphemy, she declared, "Father Lacombe is my beloved son, in whom I am well pleased." Could Brocard have heard right? Had this frail young woman co-opted the words of God the Father for her own use? And wasn't Madame de Maintenon at least appalled by such a glaring lack of humility?

Long silences were punctuated by great outpourings of words. And when these dissertations, because they were nothing short of elaborate explanations of scripture and faith, when they would come, the girls of St. Cyr would open their notebooks and scribble away. Intent on not missing a single inspired dropping.

It was curious to note how respectful Madame de Maintenon was throughout this entire display. She was a woman of quality who gained respect by giving it to others. Still, Brocard rather hoped that she would have a more critical eye for what was happening. Could it be that, as he was manifestly a man of this time, he had no way of entering into the mind of a woman, no less one of the seventeenth century? Perhaps then he would have seen how liberating Madame Guyon's very presence was — and how very explosive.

24

*P*ino had found out that there was another murder-suicide, as the accumulating bodies seemed to be, although Sophia had not been any more specific than to identify the lost soul as Jan. Zinka understood fully how poor Sophia's newfound obsession had confused her thinking. After all, Camille herself, cool to a fault, got quite distracted while worshiping Zinka's private parts. It was perfectly understandable that Pino's charms would have had a similar effect on Sophia. Nevertheless, such vagueness hampered her investigation — and displeased her mightily.

She was encouraged however by being given permission to enter the Inner Sanctum of Initiates, which meant that she would be able not only to observe Natalia better but also get a deeper understanding of the workings of her sect. Interestingly, these Bowl Services, as they were called, took place at two in the morning — a time when most people would have to be woken from their sleep. That time when our minds are most susceptible to persuasion and least able to think critically. An intriguing tactic to take.

Wanting to make sure that she was fully alert to absolutely everything, Zinka had drunk and peed out over twenty cups of coffee since dinner. In a word, she was wired—given her normal intensity this made for a uniquely hyper-attenuated condition.

"Well aren't we one privileged little bunch," she announced to anyone who would hear as she threw back her shoulders and pushed out her tits and plopped herself down on the carpets that had been laid out. "It's amazing we all didn't get our own little thrones."

There were only eight other initiates gathered for the service, all with their heads dropped and eyes closed—all except Zinka that is, who was making mental notes of everything. The room was clouded with incense, billowing up from oversized braziers in each of the corners of the Great Hall, giving out that unmistakable odor of holy marijuana. If the hour of the night didn't get them, the grass would do the trick.

On an altar to the side of the throne, which awaited the High Priestess Natalia, was an elaborate golden bowl surrounded by concentric rings of votive candles. At one time it must have been a sacred salver to be used as one religious element for Eucharistic bread. Now, however, it stood empty and alone, in silent testimony to new ritual purpose.

With great solemnity, two heralds entered the room and raised their trumpets. Before Zinka could cover her ears—she found loud noises so distressing—they had began to blow, but the sound was muted and measured, a gentle mooing of a rhythm which announced the entry of the virgin cow herself, Natalia. Except for one tit swinging in the breeze, she might very well have been the queen at the opening of parliament, so very dignified and utterly, no pun intended, aloof. As you might well imagine, Zinka was quite impressed with her little sis as she made her way over to the bowl and elevated it ceremonially over the heads of the initiates.

"The golden bowl," she intoned, "was filled with the anger of the Universal Force, but now has been emptied into the world. As the vessel was emptied of all that is evil, so too will our bodies be purged forever more." Rather convincing really. Solemn too.

Returning the bowl to the altar the High Priestess took her place on the throne. In quiet yet deliberate tones she explained how privileged, how chosen these few initiates were. It was they who could help the Church accumulate the precious objects that needed protection from the coming plagues. And when their work was done, they were given a ticket out.

"Just as we take a train to go to a city," Natalia paused for maximum effect, "we take death to go to a star." Surely that was Van Gogh's line, Zinka thought. And why, she wondered, was she chosen to be part of the elite death squad? It wouldn't be long to wait before she would find out.

25

*T*here wasn't much that Dr. Emil Rothenberg could do to make himself attractive to the alluring and provocative Professoressa Zinka, but he was determined to give it his best try anyway. Clothes were out, as he sweated too much for silk; nor did being naked work either, as the accumulating rolls of fat around his middle had compelled his cock—a sizable asset in his younger years—to permanently retreat into the folds of flesh. And as for his once charming wit, that, it seemed had irrevocably transformed into apodeictic pomp, a liability of having been active in the Paris art world so many years. No, the only way around it was to aid Zinka in her investigation, because she fancied herself a sleuth every bit as much as sex goddess. And with his years at the Louvre, not to mention consulting both legitimate and disreputable clients, he knew just how to be of help.

After sipping his bowl of café au lait and consuming no less than four brioche, Dr. Rothenberg left his elegantly appointed apartment on the Faubourg St. Honoré, squeezed his bulk into a waiting taxi at the nearby rank and headed for the Paris offices of Interpol. Chief Inspector Michot and he had been doing each other favors for so long that they had long since forgotten whose turn it was to return a favor and simply did what they could for each other. Needless to say, he was an inestimably good friend to have in such circumstances.

"*Et bien mon vieux*," Emil began, not quite knowing how to broach the subject, "we have a situation which may or may not be critical, but which, how can I say it, requires a certain finesse, which I believe you can give to it and I, of course, will assist in as best I can."

"What is this situation you need help with my good Doctor Rothenberg?" Michot, collaborating with Americans as he did, had no problem cutting to the chase.

The combination of the early morning taxi ride, the stairway that had to be scaled to get to Michot's office, not to mention the run-on sentence with which he began their meeting, was too much for poor Emil Rothenberg. Winded and spent, he could only speak in short, intermittent spurts, but these were enough to explain the situation in Central Europe. Taking it all in, jotting notes so as to underscore his professionalism, Chief Inspector Michot devised a plan.

"From what I can gather, there might well be a plundering of church art in Central Europe which, due to bad record keeping and lack of communication from one law-enforcement to another, has not risen to the level of our organization. This situation, if I can be candid with you, has been suspected for some time but, lacking any notification of a stolen artwork, has been impossible for us to verify. Have I clearly expressed your concern?"

"Admirably." Dr. Rothenberg was delighted that the Inspector was running on his own steam, nevertheless somewhat guilty that there was not more for him to do. Zinka, after all, had to be won over. "Is there not," he added, "something I might do to help in this matter?"

"There most assuredly will be my friend, but first things first."

Starting small so as to develop policies and procedures for the entire region, the key, as Inspector Michot explained it, was getting records of all illegal breaking and entries on church properties over the decade since the fall of communism in the Western Czech Republic. Of course, if there were any reported thefts of objects, something he seriously doubted as the current records in most parishes were incomplete, these too would be added to the data base.

"The practice which developed under communism, as I am sure you are aware dear Doctor, was for the church to hide many of its treasures so that the communists wouldn't defile or loot them. The whereabouts of these paintings and ritual objects was known by one or at most two people, often a sexton since most rural parishes had no resident clergy." Then walking around to the front of his desk and leaning towards Emil, Inspector Michot, gave Dr. Rothenberg his marching orders. This was one of those times when Dr. Rothenberg did so wish that his body would cooperate. But given his enormous bulk, he was not able to lean forward to show his concern and interest. He did however manage to lift his left eyebrow ever so slightly because he was ever so interested.

"What we will need you to do is to go to the Episcopal Archives in Prague and put together a list of the treasuries of all church property which have had criminal entry. We can then inspect those churches, monasteries and rectories to see if the paintings and objects they should have in their possession, are in fact still there."

It was safe to say that the Dr. Emil Rothenberg who left the office of Interpol was a new man. There was packing to be done and letters to be written. Thank God he still had an office at the Louvre, closet though it was, and impressive letterhead on which to write the Cardinal Archbishop of Prague. Life was no longer an endless procession of rising and eating, tasty though most of his meals might be. The heart of the woman he loved lay in the wait; good might even triumph over evil. Or was it to be the other way around? Whatever the case might be, it was the fat boy's time to sing.

26

Avertanus my old friend,

There is so much I don't understand about women. Especially, I might say, those who have been dead for almost three hundred years. Perhaps I best explain.

Needless to say I was visiting St. Cyr again, that most wonderful College of Piety, where Madame Guyon had been given carte blanche to teach her decidedly heterodox Christianity. As I think of it now, teach is perhaps not the most accurate of words. Promote or expound or even exude might be nearer the reality. There she was, eyes closed, beautifully coiffed, the very model of elegance, seated opposite a class of girls in complete silence. She was not praying for them, not praying with them, but – as she explained in a few brief words – "acting as a reservoir through which grace flowed" to them. Next to her was a duchess, or so she was called when the girls had curtsied to her in unison. She said that she had been compelled to leave Paris to be in the presence of Madame Guyon so as "to drink from the well of this grace." The silence in the room gave way to moans from Madame Guyon, an unladylike bovine moo, if truth be known. In one of her earlier talks I had remembered her saying that she was often overflowing with what she referred to as a 'mysterious influence.' This, it seems, was it.

What I did not expect was that her tits – please excuse such graphic language – expanded to the size of small watermelons. Heaving up and down and growing ever larger. At this the duchess, obviously familiar with such activity, sprang up and unlaced Madame Guyon's corset. And not a moment too soon.

Needless to say, the girls, being at that impressionable age, were swept up by the erotic magic of the moment. So too was the great Fénelon. There he was, standing rigid in the back of the room, incapable of taking his eyes off the young woman with the inflatable boobs. There too was Madame Maintenon, standing off to one side and unseen by him, observing everything that was happening. She had a look on her face that I find hard to describe. At first I thought it was curiosity, then fear, than even nausea, the results of a cassoulet with too many beans. But in thinking back on it now, I think it was jealousy, an emotion which I have difficulty recognizing as to the best of my knowledge I have never experienced it.

The next moment was present to, and you will have to excuse me for jumping ahead as I never know why one scene follows on another. Nor, for that matter, how they do. It is only in retrospect that I see a purpose for this. But I'm rushing ahead. Back to the private conversation Madame de Maintenon was having with

Bossuet, who you and all Church historians know best as Fénelon's nemesis.

"Madame," Bossuet said making a bow so profound that he had difficulty righting himself, "I am honored to be in your service."

"As Bishop of Meaux and a theologian of undisputed orthodoxy, you are the advisor we need to assure that the ladies of St. Cyr do not fall into heresy.'

"They are gentle creatures," I remember Bossuet saying in the most unctuous of tones, "delicate flowers that need protection from the buffeting winds." He was a bloated little man, Bossuet, rather peasant-like. It seemed to me he was filled with gas, if you'll excuse my rather candid observation. There was also something of the self-righteous opportunist in him. You could tell he was pleased as punch to be in such courtly surroundings, being treated so deferentially.

Madame Maintenon, au contraire, was all composure. She seemed a woman on a mission — search and destroy, that is.

"She writes incessantly you know. Well, dictating is more to the point, as laying pen to paper seems beneath her. I've heard a little of what she dictates and it seems highly inflammatory.' Then, easing herself into an ornate armchair in that style which her husband had made all the rage, she said in a firm whisper of a voice, "the woman must be stopped. She simply must be."

"Madame will excuse me for being direct?"

"Please," she said raising her hand towards him so that he would kiss deferentially, "you have my permission to advise without reservation."

"We must stop this false prophetess now, route her out. Two things can and must be done immediately, if you but give the word."

Madame de Maintenon leaned forward in her chair and the glance she fixed on him was nothing short of gleeful. Without saying a word, she waved her hand to signal that she wanted her pet cleric to dance to her tune.

"Her papers, all of them, no matter how personal they might be, no matter where they are hidden, must be confiscated and inspected thoroughly." Then sidling up to Madame, he leaned over and said with icy determination, " and she must be seized, placed under house arrest, so that she can do no more harm."

Then something peculiar happened, a reversing of tables, or so at least it seemed. Madame cast an upwards glance at the Bossuet, Bishop of Meaux and said in the most beseeching of tones, "your blessing father."

"My child," he said as he stood over her and placed his hands on her head. And I noticed as he sliced the air in cruciform that Madame de Maintenon's lips seemed to mouth the name of Fénelon.

Do you see what I mean my friend? How is anyone to make sense of all this? Not that Madame Guyon was a saint – I think her a bit of a charlatan if truth be known – but she doesn't deserve this. The confiscation of all of her papers. Arrest. It all seems a bit severe, a bit too overdrawn. Then again it is the Court of Louis XIV. Might be that this is perfectly normal behavior. Disquieting though.

Your friend,

Brocard

27

*T*t goes without saying that sex is far more exciting when it is shrouded in danger. Who among us, after all, doesn't long to have a dalliance in a car racing down a motorway, or in the room next door to a mother or wife? But even the most mundane of activities, like checking your e-mail, can take on an undeniable frisson when discovery might bring peril. The Church of the Age of Doom dissuaded communication with the outside world ostensibly on spiritual grounds. No letters, no telephone calls and no clandestine meetings in cyberspace. But Zinka, being Zinka, never understood the word 'no'.

It was easy enough for her to charm the librarian, a lackluster anemic with masochistic tendencies, into allowing her to log onto the only computer with a modem when no one was around. Zinka's ploy was she had to check in on her investments, a far more compelling lie than a dying relative. For most of us at least, money trumps heart.

What drove Zinka to log on was her sense of responsibility, an often-dormant trait that reared its ugly head from time to time. The fact was that she had not heard from her girlfriend Camille in quite some time. Not that, if truth be known, she really missed her. She had the well-hung Pino and the beauteous sister Natalia to distract her. Not to mention dozens of willing slaves that longed to sit at her feet, or wherever else she chose to put them. But Camille was her companion, after all, and even though the lust had long since left their relationship, their lives were connected. She felt at the very least that she should find out what had happened to the girl. Hopefully, she thought as she typed up the address and began her note, poor Camille had not gone the way of her parents and been splattered on the tarmac by some eighteen wheeler. Zinka was, after all, far too young to be a widow — far too lively in spirit to wear black.

However she had not gotten far, hardly moved beyond the gratuitous words of longing, when she heard a rustling behind her (chiffon, she thought, but it might well have been toile), she went off line and swung her chair away from the screen.

"Was someone being a naughty girl?"

"I've been accused of everything from malicious to nasty," Zinka said beaming the most radiant of smiles, "but no one has ever dared call me naughty before."

"Dare, I do," Natalia purred making her way over to Zinka's side and standing alluringly above her, "and dare I will." Then, in the most fluid and natural of gestures, she placed her hand beneath Zinka's chin, gently raised her massive head, and planted a kiss on her lips. "You remind me of someone I knew," she said warmly, smiling almost as if she new the secret.

"Is this right?" Zinka knew the words sounded hollow. That her questions about what constitutes incest had to remain hidden; that for Natalia, there were no laws except the ones that she herself promulgated. Still, her heart was pounding so strongly that she had to ask, again, so softly that it carried little weight, "Is this right?"

"You're here for a purpose, you know." Natalia toyed with a lock of Zinka's hair every bit as willfully as she was with her mind. "I'm using you. Might even say, I need you, my dear."

"Your willing slave," Zinka said with a smile. But she quite seriously meant it as her eyes roved from the plunging cleavage to the sultry eyes of her priestess baby sister. In truth, she had found that old time religion—had been struck and pinned down by Artemis.

"I have art, you know, beautiful objects, wonderful paintings."

"I've seen a few, here and there." Zinka was trying to be vague but she found it impossible to hide anything from Natalia. And longed to gain her confidence.

"What I want from you, is your eye and your knowledge," Natalia cooed.

"Why not take my body while you're at it?" Zinka was nothing if not direct.

"All in good time, my darling." Her hauteur made her even more desirable—she was impossible to resist. "Right now, I need you to catalogue and appraise, like a good little girl."

"How did you know that I was an art historian?" Zinka asked.

"Call it divine wisdom, if you will," she said in the most assured of tones. "Just do it."

From that moment on Zinka was not herself, as anyone who has been a slave to passion knows all to well. Others would have to do her work for her. Fortunately, they were all too eager to take up the challenge.

28

*G*ranted the tits were just as large, the energy just as manic and the language still as exasperatingly convoluted: fact was that this was not the same Zinka. Something had changed. In a very real way, she seemed bewitched. Even though she couldn't say what exactly it was that held her under its sway, Camille had no doubt that it was as powerful as it was real.

"You're sure you don't mind my surprising you like this?" Camille tried to be light-hearted but this was not her nature, even at best of times. "I missed you, you know."

"Well me too, my moist melon. It is so very hard being without you." Was it the flatness of Zinka's tone, or the deadness of her eyes that made Camille feel that this was a total lie?

Perhaps, Camille thought grasping at straws, her girlfriend's mind was caught up in her new task of cataloguing, authenticating and estimating the room after room of treasures this dubious Church had acquired. The ornate frames, overwrought liturgical vessels and elaborate vestments piled all around her, distracted Camille herself.

"Can I give you a hand with that?" Maybe being helpful would break the spell. She helped Zinka remove a gold monstrance from a small room off the high-ceilinged lounge that Natalia had given her for a work area.

"*Grazie.* Just place it on the credenza, will you, while I sort through these vestments."

Camille wondered if this was an invitation to follow her girlfriend into the darkened closet. What should have been so natural — following her lover into an intimate space where they might frolic at will — now seemed so artificial. Camille questioned the wisdom of coming out to Bohemia at all. And despite Zinka's assurances to the contrary, she was dreadfully nervous about being discovered by the haughty High priestess.

"Darling, it's you!" Camille gasped as the Professoressa Zinka processed into the room bedecked in cope, mitre and assorted Episcopal finery. "Turn slowly and let me feast my eyes."

But Zinka did not turn, transfixed in the role that the robes demanded. How true it is that the clothes make the man. Especially when the man happens to be a woman.

"Turning, my little pumpkin, is out of the question with

such a weight on my shoulders—not to mention my breasts." Something of her old sense of humour was trying to break through. "You can though, should you be so inclined, reverence some part of me—a hand, a foot, take your choice." It was the old Zinka, Camille thought, subdued but still irreverent and playful.

"What would have made him do it, Zinka?" Camille was down on her knees, giving mock obeisance to her liege, wondering out loud about Jan's gruesome suicide, that she had recently heard about. "Why would anyone kill themselves over objects?"

"Not objects, my moist one," she said raising her foot slightly so as to signal the next area deserving of worship, "obsession. Jan was offered the possibility of being of service to a veritable goddess, a person of such beauty that he came to life because of her attention."

Camille hadn't the slightest idea what Zinka was talking about. A dead body contorted by pain was not a witness of someone brought to new life. To insane death, surely. No more. What Camille did see though was that Zinka had lost her critical faculties. Even the fun of the clerical drag she was wearing didn't lighten her up. Maybe she needed an old fashioned tickle.

"No, you little monster." Zinka pulled her foot away from Camille's strumming fingers. "No." But it was too late. The laughter started ladylike and ended in guffaws. Then, unable to steady herself she began to wobble and, like a Sequoia being felled, careened headlong to the ground. It was only by sheer luck that frail Camille managed to avoid being squashed.

This was what Camille had been waiting for—laughter, the dropping—quite literally—of all façade and their bodies pressed up against each other horizontally. Granted a few fewer layers of flocked velvet would have made things more romantic. But beggars have to make do.

"Zinka, my dear," she said running her hands through her lovers dishevelled hair, "isn't love a lot more fun than obsession?"

"It depends on with whom, my pumpkin." Despite her unseemly posture and enforced intimacy, Zinka had regained her distance. "It all depends on with whom."

Just then Pino came into the room unannounced.

"It looks like fun down there," he said, seeing their bodies but having no idea whatsoever of the true distance between them. Undeterred by the lack of response, Pino crouched down over Camille, lively and willing to please. It was a joke, of course, even he had no illusions about rigid Camille Blanchierderie, lesbian to the core, even for a second consenting to play around with him — with any man for that sake. Still, when Camille looked into his eyes she saw complicity and enthusiasm. The exact opposite of what she saw in her one-time lover's. And she knew right then that if she was ever going to get her girlfriend back, was ever going to get to the bottom of these murders and thefts, she was going to have to sleep with the devil. Figuratively at least.

"Come on," she said to Pino as she raised herself from the floor. Then, without as much as a glance back to the pile of hierarchical garb on the floor, she told him, "we, at least, have work to do. And no time to spare."

29

*J*t was a place that triggered an emotion in him of unbearable intensity. Granted Bertie was always a sensitive soul — his mom had always said that back in Bradford, "such a delicate little flower my Bertie" she would say — still nothing had prepared him for feelings of this magnitude. The Castle of the Church of the Age of Doom (or Apocalypse Now, as he was wont to call it) was every bit as dank, massive and oppressive as the Monastery of San Redempto, his home in Rome for so many years, had been. And, of this he had no doubts whatsoever, it was equally as doomed.

Structurally the building sagged and bulged, an exhausted pile whose time had long since gone. Several of the rooms that abutted the hill into which it was built had already been boarded up because their outside walls had collapsed, allowing mud and debris to consume them. But it was more than this. Deception clung to every surface; perversity hid in every crevice. It was, in a word, evil: a breeding ground for distortions and untruths, for delusions and deceit.

Priest that he was, defrocked in the Church's eyes but never his own, he found the quasi-religious structure of the Church of the Age of Doom nothing short of blasphemous. Initiates, monastic tunics, chants, hierarchies of piety – it was all too much for him to stomach. Then again, he thought as he made his way down the central corridor, what was Christian religious life if not a plundering of pagan forms? And pagan religious practices if not a plundering of atavistic rites whose origins were lost in time? Religions cannibalise so as to live; plunder so as to grow. So why should this Church be any exception? Why should it literally nauseate him? Surely it was more than the Castle it was in – mouldy and unpleasant as it surely was.

The Castle was quite simply a visual metaphor for the rot he saw all around him. Which enveloped him like a noxious cloud, in which it was not possible to draw breathe. The only good people he could find were the weak ones, whose reality had been so compromised, whose self-worth had been so debased that they were mere shadows – ineffectual spectres. But it was to one of these spectres he had decided to go, in an attempt to get some answers.

"Sister Sophia?" Pino's slave – because that was what she had become – turned white with fear at the sound of her name. "May I have a word with you, please?"

Years of clerical privilege had trained Bertie well. When he needed to, he could intimidate with a look and command with the most innocuous of words.

"Well, yes, of course, if you want to speak with me, of course." Sophia looked both ways to make sure no one was watching them and then signalled for Bertie to follow her into a niche in the ambulatory where they would not be seen. "How may I help you?"

This gratuitous use of titles like 'brother' and 'sister' troubled Bertie After all, to be a Sister or Brother in the Catholic religious world from which he came involved years of spiritual exercises. Not just an excursion ticket from Prague and a change of wardrobe. Still, it was information that Bertie was after. He was prepared to play whatever game was necessary so as to obtain it.

"Who is the King? And how do I get to talk with him?"

Sweat pooled from Sophia's brow and her hands began to shake under Bertie's gaze. Try as she might, she was unable to speak, so overwhelming was the demand.

For several days Bertie had been struggling to find out from whom the High Priestess Natalia derived her authority. As anyone Roman trained knows all too well, authority can be snatched or conferred but it always must be derived. Something has to stand behind it, a tradition or—as he had suspected for some time must be the case in the Church of the Age of Doom—knowledge or information that would hold everyone in its power. It was Pino who first came up with the name King, a quasi-mythic figure who was related to the founder, but little more. Then Camille heard Zinka make mention of the King (as casual as she could make such a title), then catch herself as if she had said too much. Even to her lover with whom she had always been so open.

"Listen, worm," Bertie said in an almost masculine tone, "if you want to keep blowing my boyfriend you had better give me an answer. Now."

"The memory." Sophia was barely audible, as if she was struggling to regain her voice. "He was there when the founder got the prophecies, was there when the Church moved to the castle, was there when the Priestess succeeded to the throne. The King is the memory of the Church."

"How do I get to meet him?" Sophia had turned mute again. "What does he like—boys? Girls? What?"

"The Pontifex Maximus is beyond sex."

Bertie had heard that before. Still if the King was not into sex, the best one to handle him would be Camille. Prudish, not a hint of genitalia and too intellectual to be thought of as sensual.

"Be a good girl and tell me where I can find this King, will you? And I'll do my part and send Pino your way. But not," Bertie said in the most ominous of tones, "until I hear from you."

Sophia scurried on her way as Bertie considered what he was getting himself into. He had begun to loathe Camille, who, improbable as it might seem, he saw as the first true threat. As Pino was a slut, sex in itself was never a concern—he would always do it and the people with whom he did it would change as readily as underwear. Which in Pino's case was not daily but frequent enough. No, Camille was a different sort of animal: almost matronly in her poise, sexless in her demeanour. She possessed all of the qualities that up until now only Bertie had supplied—fiscal responsibility, organisational skills and the ability to put up with literally anything. This last, a legacy of years of relationship with Zinka. The fact that Camille loathed anything remotely masculine was of no concern to Pino and, in fact, made her more desirable still in his eyes—a veritable Everest waiting to be scaled, if only one survived its frigidity.

Ultimately, Pino thought that he had one objective only: to identify the root of the evil at work in this most sinister of places. Everything else, from the pettiness of jealousy to the piling up of corpses, was mere backdrop. No one he had yet met and nothing he had yet seen could explain the diabolic force at work. His suspicion and fear was that the King, who this was, held the answer.

30

*B*rocard was tiring of her schoolgirl ways, but not her theories. In fact, the dreaded thoughts of her ebullient squeals and cliched speech—let's not go there—dissolved into nothing as soon as she spun her tales of Madame Guyon.

"It must have been awesome to have been there when she was giving birth," then, realizing she had not been clear enough, Judy added, "spiritual birth, I mean, you know?"

"Was there a breaking of the holy water?" Brocard suggested, trying to be coy.

"Well, no, everything but." Judy had not caught on, but forged ahead. "You know, like contractions that she said came from her heart and womb. And screaming, lots of screaming. She would like writhe around on the floor and sweat and scream. And then when it was over, when she was being cradled by the midwives—some countesses usually, you know—she would claim someone as her spiritual child. And that was that."

"Awesome," Brocard confirmed, in as convincing a tone as he could muster. But 'outrageous' is what he truly thought, as from what he had read these specially chosen Spiritual Children became, in reality, her virtual slaves. Although, for them, it seems, the privilege far outweighed the responsibility.

"If they were ever in trouble, you know like had any crisis," Judy said, fingering her hair obsessively, "they had only to cry out for her and she would be there in spirit to rescue them." Then, entering into it, she flopped around on the floor and yelped, "*Ma mère! Ma mère!* I'm drowning!" Or, she said, rising to her knees, "*Ma mère!* The building, she is burning! And, zap, there she is, like God almighty, to the rescue."

"And the really neat thing is," Judy continued, returning to her chair, "the glorious Madame Guyon did this in full view of her salon. It was theatre, don't you see? Neat, huh?"

"Well, it is not as if they saw her rescue someone from a burning building or pull them out of the rapids, is it?" Brocard's tone was deliberately subdued, his manner controlled, in a vain attempt at dampening Judy's unbridled enthusiasm. But she would have none of it.

"No don't you see?" she said, springing up from her chair. "It didn't matter what happened. All that mattered was what people thought happened. And they got so caught up in what she said she could do that they wanted to believe that she did it. That she was a Spiritual Mother. That she was a channel to God if not God Herself."

If there were any way of telling Judy how he had seen this for himself, how he, Father Brocard Connors living in the Twenty-First Century had physically been in the same room and experienced Madame Guyon and her Salon in the Seventeenth Century, he surely would have. But as effusive and eager as she was, Brocard felt that even Judy McCabe would not be able to accept this. So he held his tongue. Still, as she read from her latest research and squealed with glee, Brocard closed his eyes and recalled an episode from his visit with Madame Guyon just the night before. One that wouldn't make it into the thesis, but that offered proof of Judy's point fully.

He found himself propped up against the cold marble walls of St. Sulpice in Paris, during one of those endless sermons that the Oratorians proscribed for daily devotion. The preacher loomed above the congregation in an elaborately appointed pulpit that encouraged bombast. Spread out at his feet, in orderly rows of chairs as this was long before pews had become the rage, was the well-heeled congregation. The silks, satins and furs were all the more luxurious in being subdued in color. Grey and faun abounded.

"It is," the fiery preacher harangued, "the healing grace of the Sacrament, and that alone, that will save you from your sinfulness and restore you to God's love."

"Non!" A woman growled from the congregation below as all eyes turned to her. Then, raising herself as majestically as any monarch, Madame Guyon extended an arm upward toward the preacher and pointed an accusing finger. "*Mon fond le rejette!* My soul rejects what you say!"

As the congregation gasped, Brocard made a rapid translation in his mind. The very ground of her being, the privileged locus where God and the mystical theology of early modern France met, rejected what the preacher had put forth. And as he fumbled to explain himself, Madame Guyon repeated her damning words, with ever increasing assurance, until finally he was silenced. There was no need for her to mount the steps of the pulpit that he had abandoned because, in truth, she had taken the pulpit on herself.

"Are you listening to me?" Judy's shrill voice wrenched Brocard from his thoughts. "I thought, like I had lost you or something," she said pulling herself up in her chair as if she were ready to make a momentous announcement. Which indeed she was.

"I think Louis XIV was pulling the strings all the time," she said in the most conspiratorial of tones. "Not that she, Madame Guyon that is, knew it. In fact, I think she was so caught up in herself that she never knew she was being manipulated like this."

"But why?" Brocard said, unable to grasp fully what Judy was telling him. And in no way aware of how this same dynamic was playing itself out in the Castle of Doom at that very moment.

"What use would such a powerful person have with a delusional woman? If you will allow me to be so direct."

"It was just another one of his ways at getting back at the system he hated."

"Which was?" Brocard asked, realizing that by now his student was playing his master.

"The Catholic Church, of course: all of those Jesuits and clerics who were forever judging him; and, those Jansenists who were forever parading their virtue over his human vices. Their power was in the sacraments. Into filling the faithful with fear, you know — scaring them shitless, so to speak Father — so that they came to them on their knees."

Suddenly Brocard saw the logic of what she was saying. And it made perfect sense. "Madame Guyon saw herself as above the sacraments, she neither needed nor wanted the mediation of priests and the church so..."

"So she made priests and the church useless, don't you see?" Judy was triumphant. And, quite possibly right. Although Madame Guyon was feared and loathed by the Church, she ultimately was not touched. And in a very real way, her power mounted with each assault the church launched against her. It was as if she was upheld by a higher power. And unless one was prepared to say she was sustained by God, which few if any these days would probably do, who better than the great Sun King Himself.

Later that evening, Brocard poured himself an Irish cream and read the following passage from Judy McCabe's developing thesis. Needless to say, he understood its meaning in a fuller and far more shocking way.

The process that Bishop Bossuet set up to review Madame Guyon's private papers was known as the *Commission of Issy*. Interestingly it began in 1694, the year Voltaire, the most damning critic of Madame Guyon, was born. Although he was not part of the Commission of Issy, as it was called, Fénelon provided a great deal of material to argue her cause. Being a great confident of the King, this tutor of Louis XIV's grandson and shortly to be named Archbishop of the See at Cambrai, two prestigious positions, gave great weight to his arguments. The extracts from orthodox mystics on mental prayer and contemplative union with God he gathered to argue Madame Guyon's cause, served as the basis for his controversial book, *Maximes des Saints* (1697).

31

*W*hy was it that Bertie was incapable of jealousy? Someone with a smattering of psychology had once told him that he had such an aggrandized personality that there was simply no way that the feelings of insecurity and low-self esteem that foster jealousy could take hold in him. However Bertie himself looked on this deficiency in the most benign of ways. He chose to believe that it had something to do with a highly enlightened permissiveness that he had spent years—and many fruitless affairs—cultivating. Whatever the case, the situation in which he now found himself was a test of openness that few children of the sixties could pass.

It was obvious to all that Zinka was so strongly under Natalia's sway that she could no longer be relied upon to lead the investigation. Pino played his part, to be sure; as did Camille in her own mousy way. But the vacuum was real and threatened to destroy all they had already done to break this case. Into that vacuum, Father Bertie, defrocked priest and ardent lover, jumped. Someone had to put all of the pieces together; make sense of this elaborate puzzle. Fortunately for him, and for us, there was an arras behind which he could snoop to his heart's content.

You remember the devise, of course? Those tapestries behind which Polonius and other Elizabethan characters intent on getting to the bottom of things hid? There were practical reasons for castles having such hangings, not the least of which was retaining some heat and muffling some sound. And aesthetic reasons, as well, like adding a bit of color and life to funereal gray halls. Still, it was their unrivaled ability to conceal passages and hide snitches that have endeared arrases to cultured minds.

Fortunately Bertie was in good shape. Remarkably so, in fact, for a man in his fifties who had never exercised and who had no interest in dedicating himself to a dietary regime. High metabolism and good genes were probably largely the reason why he had weathered the ravages of time so well. His mum back in Blackpool still had a trim little figure and a perky arse, if he didn't say so himself, at age 75. However, being a monk at heart, if not in daily practice, Bertie was convinced his physical well being could be laid at the feet of prayer. Or, at the least, a silent block of time that he carved out of every day as faithfully as a gourmand did his food. Or a nymphomaniac her dalliances. Just sitting quietly with himself and occasionally his God bathed him in an aura of peace that did wonders for his stress level. To say nothing of his complexion.

Bertie slipped behind the arras in the Great Hall just as he heard Pino and Sophia entering for a meeting Pino had told him they were to have. Never losing that boyish look, Bertie was thin enough to be able to move behind the tapestry without causing it to flutter—the give-away that got poor Polonius skewered by Hamlet. Carefully he worked his way along until he found a worn patch that afforded him a reasonably good view of the proceedings. Exhibitionist slut that he was, Bertie knew well that Pino, the love of his life, would not take offense at being spied on. As for Sophia, Bertie didn't give a damn.

"Over here," Pino commanded the shriveling Serb who from the look in her puppy eyes longed for nothing more than to be treated as if she were nothing. "Down on the floor when you talk to me." Then raising his voice as if to a recalcitrant dog and pointing his finger to his feet, Pino bellowed, "Get down now." This was not the Pino that Bertie snuggled up to at night. But he had to admit it was quite a convincing persona.

"It is important information, I promise," Sophia simpered from below.

"If you want the drink," Pino said grasping his crotch and scowling down at the simpering fool, "it had better be good."

Sophia was too transfixed by the slow movement of Pino's fingers up to the zipper, that she went mute. Leaning over it, Pino grasped Sophia by the hair and snapped her head up so that she was forced to look him in the eyes. "Is it good enough for the drink? Is it?"

"Yes, sir," Sophia stammered. Then, catching herself,

added, "nothing is that good, sir, but it is maybe important."

"We'll see," Pino said releasing his grasp on Sophia's hair and turning his back on her. "We'll see if you've got enough information to pay for it."

Through the weave of the tapestry Bertie could see Sophia raise herself slightly from the floor, collect her thoughts, cast a look over her shoulder to make sure that no one was there, then quietly begin.

"Two things," she began deliberately, "there are two things that have happened." Sophia paused to see if Pino would turn around, but it was obvious that she would have to speak to his back. Bertie, however, could see his boyfriend's face. It had a cold and calculating smirk on it that he found curiously appealing. Once a hustler, always a hustler, Bertie realized. And what a pro Pino was.

"You know the side entrance, the one by the hillside?" It was clear that Pino was not going to respond so Sophia continued, "there has been a lot of activity there the past day. A truckload of paintings, sculptures, old vestments and chalices, you know, was unloaded. And then almost immediately a truckload of things in crates were brought out." Not knowing if this was enough, but intent on getting her point across, Sophia added. "This is important." Then crawling tentatively towards Pino, "we never had a full truckload come before and in all my time here I never, never heard of anything leaving." Silence. "Please," Sophia whimpered, "you said I could if it were important."

Bertie watched as Pino slowly unzipped his trousers. Even flaccid, it was impressive. Then without a word being spoken he turned and Sophia crawled over and took it in her mouth.

The fact that the love of his life was peeing into a woman's mouth, unusual and distasteful as this might be, was not what disturbed Bertie. What unsettled him most was how tender this act was. How used to this undeniably intimate act both of them had become. Not a drop was spilt as Sophia gulped and raised her tear filled eyes to Pino for more. Not a word was exchanged, nor did it have to be, as one fed on the other. As both, presumably, had their deepest sexual and psychological needs met. Perhaps Bertie was making too much of it. Nevertheless, it seemed to him that he was observing a secret ritual, a primal act, which unconditionally excluded him.

Just then there was a tapping on the door and a discrete rattling of the knob. Quicker than an Irishman's fuck, Pino pulled himself out of Sophia's mouth. It seems they had finished their little drinking ritual, and even more unsettling for Bertie to observe, were simply hanging out, attached. Pino zippered his fly and signaled for Sophia to hide — of all places — behind the arras.

Bertie, of course, was shocked to see Sophia sliding behind the tapestry and edging her way along the wall. But his shock was nothing to compare with Sophia who realized in a heartbeat that an outsider had witnessed her little piss-drinking escapade. As their eyes met, Bertie put a finger to his mouth to tell her to keep quiet; Sophia, for her part, put a finger to her mouth to catch a final drop that lingered at the corner of her mouth and managed an embarrassed smile. Fortunately neither of them could say anything, as there was nothing to say.

"Camille, my princess," Pino said as the plain looking librarian made her way towards him. Charm seems to be given Italians of any class as a birthright. Kissing Camille's hand, he moved closer to her and ever so gently placed his hand on her crotch. This, too, shocked Bertie even more than he had expected. What self-respecting dyke, he wondered, would allow herself to be felt up by a man? And an Italian, at that?

Not that Camille had any clear idea of why she permitted such intimacy. Novelty, perhaps, which definitely had its limits, should Pino have tried to force himself on her. Or maybe it was to see what made Zinka periodically attracted to such creatures. Could it have even been to enflame jealousy in her girlfriend's heart? Any intense emotion works when relationships go stale, as it seems theirs had. Whatever the case, she allowed Pino to rub away as she told him about Zinka's most recent findings.

"There is a group of lactating virgins, that's the Baroque trope, as you no doubt are aware." Camille squirmed a bit, the boy definitely needed to clip those nails. "The lot of them are Bohemian: Breitl, Skreta, Liska — all the great names."

In the midst of her catalogue, someone could be heard entering the hall from the far door. Not wanting to be seen, especially in such a compromising situation, Camille made a run for the armoire, which she got into just in time for Pino to close the door behind her and turn to see the man who had entered.

Bertie broke out into a cold sweat. He had not known his worst nightmare until it stood in front of him. For Sophia, this was a rare and treasured occasion to see the man who she thought could only be the King, the master behind the Church of Doom. As for Pino, no man — no matter how perverse or evil — had the power to unsettle his composure, which was based on the unshakable knowledge that his sexuality was universal and not to be resisted.

"Curious creature," the elderly man said, making his way over to Pino. "Turn," he ordered him spinning his hand as if to a trained animal, "turn and let me see you."

Accustomed as he was to being inspected like meat, Pino turned slowly around for the gentleman, once, twice and three times, locking eyes with him as if to gain control. Who, Bertie thought, was the lion after all? And who the tamer?

"Natalia, the Priestess, has not mentioned you to me. I'll have to reprimand her," he said, smacking his lips. "Now, run off and I'll call for you when I need you."

"Don't you want to know my name?" Pino asked in a tone that was as defiant as it was submissive. That slut, Camille thought, from her airless armoire. Hustler, slut.

"You don't need a name," the lecherous old man retorted, "an object like you won't be hard to find."

Pino barely gave a thought to Sophia behind the arras and Camille in the armoire as he scurried out of the hall. In time, when the coast was clear, they would crawl out of their respective holes. It was Bertie who was frozen in fear and unsettled beyond all speaking. A ghost from the past had come back to haunt him and doubtless cause no end of trouble.

Bertie's mouth formed the name that he most dreaded in this world. "Otger," it said soundlessly. "Otger."

32

Avertanus, my dear friend,

Would that I knew how to begin. Failing any warm wishes and regrets for being out of touch, let me cut to the chase (as Hollywood directors used to say, but there's me being pedantic again). Anyway: Otger has surfaced. More to the point, it seems he well might be behind this mess that Zinka finds herself in, out there in Bohemia.

Here is what has transpired. You knew, I believe, that Father Bertie and his lover Pino left their love nest in the Abruzzi to join Zinka in her investigation at the Castle of Doom some time ago. Well, to make a long story short, there was some rumor about a "king", some Oz-like figure who was pulling the strings behind the scenes (is that a mixed metaphor?). Anyway, Bertie was hiding behind an arras (don't ask, just stay with me here.) Who should he see, identified as the 'king' himself by the degenerate with whom he was sharing the tapestry (let's not go there)? No other than Father Otger Aarnick himself, the bane of our existence when we were in religious community together at San Redempto in Rome. And if I am not mistaken, someone who was supposed to be enjoying his retirement up in Nijmegen with you, in your House of the Dead.

Need I remind you how sadistic and, undoubtedly murderous, he was and presumably still is? If there is evil incarnate, it is surely our Father Otger. Supposedly he is still as elegant and composed as the devil himself. But why, if you don't mind my asking, is he in the Czech Republic when he is supposed to be with you in Holland? Not that I am asking you to be your brother's keeper. But then again, maybe I am.

Nothing any of us can do about this at all. Except pray.

Yours, Brocard

My dear overwrought Brocard,

So that is where Otger has been escaping to on his extended trips outside the cloister. As you might remember, Dutch law protected him from being extradited to France on charges brought in the St. Agatha affair. They were, as you surely recall, quite substantial charges indeed, ranging from grand larceny to conspiracy to commit murder. With the borders down throughout Europe, it is easy work for him to head west through Germany, then south to Bohemia. What a treasure trove of stolen art works he might be able to assemble in that rich, lawless and greedy corner of the continent.

Your most interesting observation, from my perspective at least, is how suave and appealing Otger was and still is. Those are not your exact words, I know, but that is how I read them. Your description reminded me of the earliest way in which the devil was depicted. The most beautiful of angels, fallen though he might be, was always believed to be beautiful in figure and manner. Because evil, after all, attracts us. It was only centuries later, during the Medieval Period, that the devil got those warts, that tail and those horns. Because of what evil does to us who fall prey to it, distort and disfigure us horribly. So, you see, elegant and composed — those were your words — suits Otger, the devil, fine. In fact, they are eminently appropriate attributes.

My only suggestion is that you be in regular contact with Bertie and Zinka. Reminding them that what might have seemed a game has now turned deadly serious. We know from experience that blood will flow in profusion should anything thwart Otger's evil designs.

You remain in my prayers.

Avertanus

33

*W*ere it not for the hills and interminable stairs, Prague would have been Dr. Emil Rothenberg's favorite European City. However given his bulk and a total repulsion to exercise of any type, Prague's endless visual charms so often eluded him. This was not, fortunately, the case, as he took his morning café au lait on the terrace of the Four Seasons. The Moldau River, he never could bring himself to call it the Vltava, made its way sluggishly under the Charles Bridge, adorned with its shrines and statues, one more splendid than the next. Sleepy Kampa Island, a sliver of elegantly appointed real estate and tempting little eateries where he had so often dined quite nicely. Someone of a more sober nature would have recalled that it was not that long ago when this very river coursed savagely over its banks, submerging Kampa and much of the Jewish Quarter adjacent to his hotel. But Emil was not of such a nature. His mind was fixed on where he was to lunch later that day and, more importantly, what he would order.

As he slathered butter on his brioche, a habit he picked up in America and thought most wonderful, he reflected on the delightful Camille. How was it that he had not noticed her charms until just recently? The simple answer was Zinka's knockers, of course. Nor would he be the last man to be blinded by such protuberances. But not to have seen the arch of Camille's neck, wrinkled though it might be, or the delicate turn of her bony ankles until now, was a remarkable oversight for someone of his exalted taste.

His taxi made its way sluggishly up the narrow, windy streets to the castle mount, clearly laboring under the weight of its cargo. It sputtered to a stop on the northern side of Hradčany Square alongside the Castle, one of the more beautiful open spaces in Prague. Before him stood his destination, the Palace of the Archbishop, with its wide sumptuous porch, Rococo pediments, splendid entablatured coat of arms, and, yes, daunting stairs.

"Dr. Rothenberg, please," an eager young cleric said opening the door. From the tired look around his eyes, Emil could see that he had been waiting quite some time. Not that this concerned him overly, just an observation, nothing more.

"His Excellency the Archbishop sends his regrets, but he was summoned to the President's office this morning." Then, catching himself, the embarrassed young man added, "no, they asked for the pleasure of his company." His voice trailed off, filled with the sad realization that, try as he might, he would never get things right.

French to the core, Emil Rothenberg lamented the loss of French as the universal language. Everything was English these days. Even in the Episcopal Court in Prague. And such rudimentary, unpolished English at that. Worse still, he himself was held hostage to this alien tongue whenever he traveled outside the borders of his native country. It was, indeed, a tragic fate to endure.

The elevator that bore Emil up to the primo piano was nothing short of a wrought-iron coffin. Still, a little claustrophobia was far preferable to having to lumber up the staircase, as impossibly vertiginous as it was grand. Quite simply, being a sleuth tried every fiber of his being.

None of this amounted to anything when Dr. Emil Rothenberg saw the work that had been done for him by the Bishop's archivists. There laid out on a vast table were all of the leather bound inventories of the paintings and liturgical objects that had been supplied to him by Camille. Thorough librarian that she was, Camille had given detailed descriptions of every object she could find at the Castle of the Church of Doom. And obsessively thorough as they were, the Episcopal Archivists had matched these up. All that remained for Dr. Rothenberg to do was to peruse these lists, verifying that they did in fact correspond and ask to have copies made of the appropriate pages. And, in so doing, give no hint of the fact that most if not all of this material was well known to him already.

Two things were easy for all to see. First, it was patently clear that all of these objects and paintings came from churches that no longer had a priest in residence. A few of them, it seemed, were mission churches of larger parishes, opening at best twice a year for religious celebrations. The majority, however, were forced to close for lack of clerical coverage. In all of these churches, a lay custodian or family had volunteered to be caretaker, presumably out of piety, although present situations called that into question. The second thing that jumped out at the good doctor was a fact that he was all too familiar with. Every last one of these churches was clustered in Western Bohemia, a region rich in Baroque treasures.

His course of action was clear. As he gathered up the sheaves of papers he knew that he must get some information to the local police. They should be told that theft had and presumably was still taking place. The sooner he told the authorities, the better.

Taking one last look at the gothic spires of St. Vitus as he crammed himself back into the waiting taxi, he realized with a sudden spasm of pain, that it was time for tea. He directed the driver to take him to the Celetna No. 7, his favorite café in the old town. He could taste the Ovocné Knedlíky already—rich fruit dumplings. He had determined to choose the plum because you can never go wrong with plum, swimming in drawn butter and smothered with sugar icing with ground poppy seeds sprinkled liberally on the top.

After having replenished himself, there would be plenty of time to catch the thief. Being French, and a gourmand at that, Dr. Emil Rothenberg had clear priorities.

34

*N*o one had told Father Brocard that he should not have a young woman in his room (although you would have thought that years of monastic training and common sense would have been instruction enough in such matters). All Brocard could think about was that he was waiting to hear both from Avertanus in Holland and Zinka in Bohemia, for which he had to stay close to his monitor. This meant that if Judy McCabe, the ebullient co-ed, wanted to talk with him at this present moment about her thesis, she had to come up to his bedroom. Propriety had to give way to expediency, Brocard thought with blinding naïveté. However, in the way that idiots and children so often dodge those bullets that hit the rest of us so regularly, his escape from scandal, lawsuits and perdition was all but assured.

"You see," Judy said rummaging through the papers she had deposited on his neatly made single bed, "it's all about what she called, what is it, the *Unité de la Unité*, or something like that." She squished her face up in that way that Americans often do when they want to speak 'foreign.'

"*Union d'unité*," Brocard quickly corrected her. Not even the distraction of the moment would permit him to allow such an egregious error to take place. "There's a liaison, in French, remember. *'De la'* can't be placed in front of a vowel. It just won't do. So it must be *union d'unité.*"

"Whatever," Judy mumbled, totally unimpressed by his pedantic outburst. "This Union business that she did was the way she communicated with her 'favorite souls,' that's her way of talking about it. Neat, huh?"

The only instant communication that Brocard was interested in was electronically hearing from Zinka, whose recent behavior was troubling to say the least. In a word, the usually trustworthy Professoressa had lost focus. Her identity, defined as much by her sense of mission as the surgical removal of her penis, seemed lost in her fascination with the High Priestess Natalia. Who was not, of course, just any priestess, but a blood-sister that obviously didn't recognise Zinka as her long lost brother Milorad because — like so many before her — she was blinded by his or rather her newly minted breasts.

As Judy spread both her thesis and herself out on the bed, a noxious little voice on the computer announced that Brocard "had mail."

"Please excuse me," Brocard said as he swivelled around to face the screen.

"Whatever," Judy mouthed voicelessly, too intent on her research to be concerned.

Eager to hear what she had to say for herself, he double clicked on Zinka's missive.

Carissimo Brocard mio padre favorito,

Forgive me for being such a naughty girl. You must have thought I had forgotten you, or, worse still, abandoned our common mission to catch the crooks, aright the wrongs — or whatever it is we do together, you and I. No need to trouble yourself on my account. All is well, quite well, and things are very much on target. However, it seems as if the target might well have changed, my darling little cleric. Allow me to explain.

First, just so that you know everything as well you should, there is art here. But nothing to warrant our concern. Minor works from an art historically provincial part of the world. Bohemian Baroque has not made an impact on the international art auction scene. Truth be known, I rather doubt if Christie's or Sotheby's consider it worthy of catalogue space. So monetarily, at least, we are not talking grand larceny.

But is theft involved at all? After all, these objects and paintings were freely given to the faith community here as love offerings. Granted, you might make the argument that these paintings and objects belonged to the church and not those people who donated them. But who is the church, after all, if not the people? And, for the fifty years religion was suppressed by the communists, where was the hierarchy? Who lit the fires in the churches to keep them from being consumed by mildew, my dearest cleric? Who hid the paintings and liturgical items so that they would be safe? Who, after all has a better right to these items than the sacristans and sextons, unpaid but loyal, without whom the buildings would have gone to ruin and the paintings would have been stolen or destroyed?

What right do we have to judge their decision? I ask myself, wondering as I do if I have not lost my critical edge. And I also ask myself how I can possibly question the faith of another, knowing how personal such choices are. What right do I have to say that Catholicism is better than this new religion being forged by my gorgeous sister Natalia? Who I truly have come to believe is goodness itself.

Now, my bald little pumpkin, I know you. What you are thinking is that Zinka's crotch is thinking again. And maybe you have some reason in thinking so. But, really, how can we go on with this Inquisition? Perhaps it is time we let this business go and simply let people do and think as they believe.

Awaiting your response – not that anything you will have to say will sway me – I remain, stubbornly and lovingly yours.

> *Zinka*

There was no time to spare. No time to reflect on how best to respond to Zinka, to worry over phraseology or trouble himself with subtle arguments. Brocard knew that Zinka had to be brought back to her senses. His sincere hope was that she was still at her computer and his message to her would reach her immediately.

Zinka my dear Zinka.

How can it be that you no longer see wrong from right? These paintings, these liturgical items belong to the Church. To our church Zinka, the Roman Catholic Church. No moral reason can be advanced that the ownership of these precious items was transferred from the organization of the church to their caretakers. They belong to the whole church, Zinka, surely you can see that.

And as to their value, who but some art dealer (and we know so well how dubious their lot can be) would ever attach a dollar value to religious art? They have worth because of how they speak to us of our God, of the blessed saints, of what we believe. That is their value — and in that, Bohemian or Parisian, they are priceless indeed.

My greatest fear, dear Zinka, is that in your need to connect with your sister Natalia (and I pray we are talking Platonically) you have started down the slippery slope of accommodation. It is patently not true that all faith is the same. Two thousand years of tradition based on the Holy Word, dear Zinka, counts for more than some do-it-yourself belief system. A world religion counts for more than a lunatic cult.

My dear Zinka remember your faith. Granted you have put Catholic teaching to the test, granted you have questioned several narrowly constructed doctrines. But the fact is that, like me my dear, you are Catholic to the bone — ashes on the forehead, May crowning, Saints Anthony and Jude when you need them Catholic. Never forget this dear child — if you don't mind my calling you this, large as you most assuredly are. Never for a minute forget that you are Catholic. For if you do, a sadness and a rootlessness will set in, the only cure for which is a return to Holy Mother Church.

Please don't be such a wilful girl and do, do listen to Father just this once.

> *Brocard*

How relieved Brocard was to have lectured Zinka so. But sadly his efforts were in vain as she was never to receive this last email. While Brocard was writing, someone surprised Zinka at the computer, something forbidden the initiates. In her haste to escape unseen, Zinka never saw that it was Otger. He, however, saw her and the vice around her was tightened so that never again would she be able to move freely around the castle. Zinka the free spirit became Zinka the immured, without for a second realizing how sinister and frightening and how vulnerable her life had become.

The only thing pressing for Brocard was hearing from his mentor and friend, Father Avertanus. Even though he was pushing sixty, Brocard needed the grounding and the perspective that only Avertanus could supply. But the more he stared to the screen, like water that won't boil if it is watched, the less there was to see and the more frustrated he became.

Realizing there was nothing to be done but to return to the co-ed on the bed, he swivelled around in his chair to resume his conversation with Judy only to find that she was dead to the world. For Brocard this low rumbling, unladylike snore meant that she had been sleep deprived — how else to explain such a deep sleep on someone else's bed? He felt a pang of guilt at being so hard on her about her thesis, or at least not giving it the full attention her hard work deserved. It never occurred to him that this was simply the way young people sleep, profligately and erratically, and had nothing whatsoever to do with her work ethic.

"Judy," he said trying unsuccessfully to rouse her with his voice, which even now was too gentle to be effective. "Young lady," nudging her on the shoulder, "it is time to continue."

"So did you get through to your friends?" she said rubbing her eyes aggressively to wake up. "Did you all chat for a bit?"

"My friends are my business colleagues if you must know. And we write letters to each other, letters that require patience and time to say precisely exactly what we must. We don't chat, as you put it, but correspond."

"Whatever," Judy shrugged, realizing that old people were just different and that, at times, there was no understanding them.

She did hope, however, that Father Brocard would finally understand Madame Guyon, who had become not just her project but also her cause.

"What I wanted to say, to point out to you Judy," Brocard continued in his most professorial tone, "is that Madame Guyon's behaviour, which you write about well, is quite aberrant and must be identified as such."

"Like what?" Judy reacted to this as if it were a personal insult. She tossed back her greasy hair and pouted her lips, like a woman who was ready for a fight. "What for example?"

Brocard was taken aback by her attitude, but forged on. "Like the way in which she heard voices? Or said she was united with those who were separated from her, even by death?" Then, taking a page from her thesis that he had marked up but not returned to her yet, he read:

Madame Guyon communicated at great distances with some favored souls, especially the unfortunate Père Lacombe. First when he was in prison, and then after his death. Likewise, she held 'silent commerce,' for in silence we speak to the divine, with several saints, especially our Lady and St. John.

Madame Guyon's answer about all this is that the state in which she was (which she called the "union d'unité") was so unique that she could find no reference in any of the spiritual writers of the past to anything quite like it.

Then, looking up at Judy he added, "Now tell me this isn't delusional behaviour."

"Oh sure," Judy said getting on her feet, her face turning red. "Like you never heard voices or never saw yourself with someone you missed or loved and had this thing for?" realizing she might have gone a bit too far, she added, "well, someone you like a lot."

How did she know? Who told her, and more to the point, what made him so resistant to something he knew was true? When in doubt, change the subject or go slowly was his motto.

"You think there were many people at her time that had such experiences?" he asked.

"No, now I'm talking about." Judy could not believe how out of touch he was. "In the seventeenth century people were dying young, poverty was rampant and women were slaves to their husbands or lovers. Madame Guyon was a lucky rich widow so she was not overwhelmed by all of this. No it's today I'm talking about. Women and even men are freer to explore this whole dimension. We have the money and the time and the opportunity."

"In other words, you are saying that Madame Guyon was not a product of her time but rather truly ahead of her time?" Brocard could see where his student was going but as he could not deny anything she said without exposing his own incursions into the occult, he let her go.

"Exactly. Who doesn't conjure up the person they love, no matter where they may be, when they talk with them on their cell phone? Is there anyone who doesn't see and hear things that transport them to another place, because that is where their heart is? And as for channelling, who doesn't channel these days?"

Of course Judy had gone over the top with the channelling remark, but as for the rest, his silence was for her his tacit approval, and she would not be stopped.

"You see" — Judy was fully awake now and animated in that way that only very young and very intense people can be — "Madame Guyon is the woman for our time. Because she used the system, because she showed that women had the religious force needed to bring fear to the old boys club. Because," here her eyes lit up as if the truth could finally be said, "she said that God lives inside us all, men and women, and to deny that was blasphemy."

"You don't think," he rushed to ask with the quickness of a man jumping out of the way of a runaway train, "she herself was manipulated?"

"Madame Guyon? Manipulated?" The thought amused and slightly shocked Judy. "That's just plain silly." Going over to the sheaves of paper on the bed she pulled out one to read, realizing that the words she wrote were clearer than anything she could say in her present state. "Listen to this."

But perhaps most telling of all, was the story told about her that had wide circulation in Paris at the end of the century: A holy man had a vision. In it he saw a bishop and two other men and Madame Guyon in a boat; they throw her overboard and try to drown her; but she keeps bobbing up to the surface again and again and again. This, in fact, was, and may still be her destiny.

"Like it or not, Father Brocard," Judy said triumphantly, "Madame Guyon is coming up for air."

35

A burial was taking place outside his window: things were definitely going from bad to worse. Avertanus knew, as nothing was random, nothing happened outside the Plan, this was a visual metaphor for the devolving situation in Bohemia in which he had become immersed. He was both old and wise enough to realize that space and time had nothing to do with how deeply we can be drawn into another's life or critical situation. The events of 9/11 had shown that to the world, though admittedly for many souls live television transmission was key to realizing this. Everyone who saw those haunting pictures was there as the first and then the second plane struck those towers. And they were transported back to the exact moment of impact with every replay. However long before such modern aids, Avertanus knew the alchemist's tools that allowed him entry into other times and places. And as he in his monastic cell on the second floor in the retirement house of his religious community watching the filling of yet another hole in the cemetery below, he did not feel cut off from Brocard in America or Zinka in the Czech Republic. Even though he was in distant Holland, and remote Zenderen at that, this was no impediment to Avertanus's involvement in this convoluted affair. If anything, it was a challenge and an opportunity, worthy of the Emeritus Doctor of Mystical Theology that he was.

Knowing Brocard as he did, Avertanus realized that he was

impatient for a reply. In all likelihood, he was staring at the monitor, waiting to find out that he had mail. But this was too important a missive to rush. It required a clear mind and possible editing. Because of this Avertanus had not sent off what he had written the night before, but rather saved it to read and rework the following morning, when he was fully rested. And now, of course, the burial below, which decided the seriousness of the tone and gave him deeper insight into what, in fact, was happening.

Father Avertanus made an interesting picture squinting to read the words on the screen. As he never could get quite used to the trifocals that had been forced upon him, he abandoned them completely at times like this and peered intently at the screen. Monk to the core, his brown cowl was pulled up over his head to block the damp morning air that the old windows of the monastery could not keep out. The scholar's back had the slightest of humps, attributable no doubt to years spent huddled in research over books. And that aquiline nose of which he had been rather proud had grown a little longer, like the skin of his face that draped in deep furrows, giving witness to the inexorable pull of gravity. In a word, were it not for the computer he was plucking away at, he looked like a medieval monk labouring to illuminate a manuscript. However the only illumination that was to take place was his friend Brocard's. And this was how he intended to do it.

My dear Brocard,

You know me well enough, my old friend, to realize that I have chosen my words carefully, especially at times like this when there is so very much to lose and when so very much is at stake. First, let me explain why it is that you seem to have lost the ability to enter into Madame Guyon's world.

Put quite simply, my dear Brocard, you have lost the passion for it. Perhaps you remember that great maxim of Albertus Magnus: Everyone is capable of everything if they fall into a great excess. You have lost the excess, you see, that unbridled passion necessary to cross the threshold into her world.

It seems quite clear as well that you are presently in no position to regain it, at least consciously to do so. This is after all something one does apart from the will. In fact, despite the will one might say.

No, you my friend are once again held under the sway of that Amazonian charmer Zinka Pavlic. It is clear to see that there is no room for two heroines in that heart of yours. So let Madame Guyon be for the time being. She may visit you, when you let down your guard; but you can no longer visit her. If Madame Guyon has something to tell you, and I feel she well might, she will come to you.

The exact nature of these visits should not trouble you. It does not matter to what extent they are extensions of your own mind, your wish fulfilment, your self-imposed truth. All reality is that more or less anyway, as everything we hear, see and touch comes through these bodies of ours and, to a greater or lesser extent, are formed by them.

More to the point, and here I ask you to pay particular heed, you must attend to the situation in Bohemia, at the aptly named Castle of the Church of Doom. Disaster is writ large on everything you tell me about it. Zinka too I fear is in danger and needs a steady hand, something you have always been good at. Go now, Brocard. Tie up whatever loose ends you have in Pennsylvania and take the first plane you can to Prague. You will know what to do when you get there, I have no doubt about that. But do go now.

Your brother and friend,

Avertanus

Avertanus had no doubt that Brocard would dither — being Brocard how could he not? — over getting involved in such a chaotic situation. But he knew, as clearly as he could see the dirt being shoveled into the grave beneath his window, that the end was near.

36

*T*he smell of mold, a pestilent musk that clung to everything, permeated the Castle. It was there before, of course, but now it was unavoidable, as was the moisture that quite literally flowed from the walls. A foul smelling perspiration that spoke of rottenness within, like a terminal illness. Then there was the groaning of the whole structure under the weight of the mountain of mud pressing down on it. That deep sustained moan of stone, stuccoes and plaster straining to hold back destruction.

Bertie, however, was on a mission, and no sound or smell could deter him from the task he knew was his. Since Zinka had abdicated her role as queen of sleuths, blinded as she was by incestuous lust, it was up to Bertie to solve the mystery. More to the point, since he loved thinking as a couple, it was up to Pino and him to get to the bottom of the dastardliness swirling around them. Something which would not only give him the credibility he felt he needed but also help bond a relationship that—rightly or wrongly—he felt was disintegrating. It wasn't of course. Where was Pino going to go after all? But Bertie had always had low self-esteem and felt he constantly had to work at relationships. Especially love relationships with particularly attractive creatures, as his lover surely was.

"Jesu, Maria, it smells like the crap-house at the *Statione Centrale* in here," Pino said waving his arms in a vain attempt to clear the air.

"The jakes at the train station were one of your favorite haunts, as I remember." Bertie liked to play with him. In the good old days, they used to work themselves up by calling each other dirty names. Verbal foreplay they hadn't engaged in for some time.

"*Merda!*" Pino exclaimed as he jumped over a pile of mud oozing out from under the door. "How do they expect us to wear white and live in such filth?" Then, rushing to catch up with Bertie, "and where the hell are we going in such a hurry anyway?"

"Keep your voice down," Bertie called back to him in a stage whisper, so well done that it echoed down the hall, virtually announcing their presence. Fortunately the High Priestess Natalia had gathered all the initiates around her in the throne room at the far end of the Castle, so they could wander at will. Bertie planned this, of course, because he was the responsible one. Pino, being his total opposite, simply blundered through life.

"What we are doing," said Bertie coming so abruptly to a halt that Pino nearly ran into him, "is looking for that slave of yours, Sophia. I need her to identify a corpse for me."

"Oh," Pino said blankly, as if this were the most common of things. Then, trying not to betray too great an interest that might damage his super-cool persona, he asked, "which corpse might that be, then?"

"One I stumbled across this morning, not far from the room where all of the art is stored." Bertie indicated the direction, nearly slipping on a pool of mud and continued to lead Pino down the hall. "I have every reason to believe we will find Sophia there, as she seems to be the one they get to do all of the dirty work around here."

"Who is 'they'," Pino asked, moving closer to Bertie and lowering his voice.

"I love it when you whisper into my ear," Bertie said coyly, which only made Pino draw closer and take a little nibble from a lobe. "Slut," he said quietly to Pino, more as a statement of fact than anything else. "'They' is really a 'he'," Bertie said trying to regain some professional distance. "One person and one person only: Otger. I am convinced of this. Everyone else is his pawn. The only mystery here is how we are going to land him."

Pino loved Bertie's self assurance — a residue from his years as a cleric no doubt. Despite his bravado, Pino had none at all –the reason, no doubt, that made him such a good hustler. And assured Bertie was, at least about the perpetrator of the crimes.

"Remember," he continued *soto voce* as they made their way down the corridor, "I have known Otger all my adult life. He has been the plague of my existence for over thirty years." Then, seeing Pino counting on his fingers, one of his most endearing traits, Bertie slapped him quickly as a clear sign that this was not an opportunity for Pino to calculate Bertie's age — something he had always been careful to conceal from his young boyfriend. With his shock of dark hairs and his boyish smile Bertie always looked a good twenty years younger than he in fact was. To himself, at least, if no one else — which is, after all, all that matters.

As so often happens in any relationship, Pino had stopped listening to Bertie and was happily engaged with his own thoughts. Sophia, as intense as she was submissive, could suck like a Hoover, a skill that Bertie—who was into 'kissy-kissy' (to use Bertie's expression) type stuff—was sorely lacking in. Searching out Sophia, even if she were encumbered by yet another corpse, was an excursion worth making. As Pino was happily engaged in such thoughts, Bertie prattled down memory lane.

"When I first arrived in Rome at the Monastery of San Redempto, Father Otger was the Procurator—you know, the monk who was in charge of the money. Even then, naïve as I was, I could tell he was up to no good. He had his special friends, the cute ones, who got everything. Tickets to concerts at Santa Cecilia, bottles of cologne, excursions to the beach at Ostia—whatever they wanted. The others, myself included, were lucky to get a second habit." Bertie came to an abrupt stop at the corner, peered around to make sure the coast was clear, and then signaled for Pino to follow him down the final stretch. "It's not just that I was jealous, which I admit I was, of the attention he gave others, but in seeing how sadistic he was, that I came to despise Father Otger. He was on constant alert for weakness and when he saw any, he went in for the kill. Anything, from a mispronunciation in Office to homesickness was enough to get him going. And he wouldn't stop until the offending soul was reduced to tears or left. Many a vocation had been lost by Father Otger's obsessive hounding. It was almost as if he wanted the Order to die, so hard did he make life for so many of the brothers. Only later in life, when my eyes were opened to the sinister workings of the monastery, did I come to understand how truly evil he was. He stole what he could, used whomever he needed to, hiding all the while behind a mask of religious piety. It was Otger who single-handedly drove me out into the night to find whatever solace I could." Then realizing perhaps for the first time the good that had come of this, he stopped and looked Pino in the eye. "Without which I never would have found you, my beautiful more-than-a hustler friend."

Although Pino hadn't heard a word of what Bertie had said, and had no idea why he was tearing up and getting affectionate, he was smart enough to realize that a kiss couldn't hurt.

"You are so sweet," Bertie said coming up for air, before going back for another smooch. "Such a positive sweetie." Then, going in for one more wet one, "you're thick as a brick and really don't understand half of what I say, but notwithstanding, a treasure."

"*Sì caro*," was all that Pino ever really had to say and all he offered now, knowing it would be sufficient. However, Pino sensed that this time there was more to Bertie's talk than his simply prattling on and determined he had best pay attention.

Bertie suddenly extricated himself from Pino's clutch and focused his attention on a discrete tapping at the end of the hallway. "Hello, what have we here?" He mumbled, in his best Poirot imitation. Then, taking Pino's hand, he stealthily made his way forward.

Stopping abruptly by the room from which the tapping was coming, Bertie flung open the door and with uncharacteristic assurance jumped right in. It's hard to tell who was more surprised. Sophia, as she struggled to roll a naked corpse into the fleshly constructed coffin; or Pino, as he tried to see the mouth who sucked him in a new, unflattering light. Or perhaps it was Bertie himself, who had slipped on the mud covered floor and slid headlong into the room, crashing to a stop at the coffin at Sophia's feet. The only certainty was that one of them was dead, everything else was up for grabs.

It didn't take long for Sophia to realizing that she was among friends. With Bertie, of course, she had spent that quality time behind the arras; and as for Pino, she had surely sucked her way into his heart. No, nothing to worry about with these two, she thought, so she set her squat little body to work again, laboring valiantly to push the dead body of an overweight man into the box she made for him.

"Allow me," Pino offered gallantly as he stepped over Bertie to help her with her task. "He's too heavy for you to push by yourself."

"It's not as if I can get a hernia or anything," Sophia said coyly, blushing deeply and obviously enjoying the attention. "But I would appreciate your help."

"Women get hernias," Pino offered solicitously, pressing his body against hers as they maneuvered the corpse to the edge of the table to drop it, unceremoniously, in the box. From his vantage point on the floor below, Bertie could see that his boyfriend was becoming unduly excited by this experience and decided to speak up, quickly.

"Will you two just shut up and shut up now?" Struggling to get up, with no help whatsoever from Pino he noted, Bertie floundered in the mud. "Where the hell did all of this mud come from?"

"The mountain, it just does that," Sophia said in the most matter of fact of tones. If truth be known she rather resented Bertie's intrusion. Not to mention the fact that there was work to be done.

"Would you mind telling me," Bertie asked when he righted himself, "what you are doing?"

"Disposing of this body, of course." Sophia could not stand stupidity. In fact, the patches of baldness on her thinning scalp were directly attributable to the stupidity of the world around her. "He is one of the last of the sexton's if you must know." Before wasting her time with any more nonsensical questions, she leaned into the task at hand. Another angle would perhaps suit her best, crouched down and salivating, focusing far more on Pino than the corpse. Necrophilia was definitely not for her.

The corpse landed in the coffin with a thud, face down and rump in the air. Given the amount of effort it took to get it in at all, it was to remain that way for all eternity.

"What do you mean, 'the last of the sextons?'" Bertie asked. "How many others were there?"

"Eight or nine, I reckon," Sophia said as she signaled for Pino to help her with the lid and then began nailing it shut. "Maybe more, I really can't remember."

"Listen." Bertie was starting to get annoyed, he really had to get to the bottom of this and Sophia was not being cooperative. Although he was covered in mud, although his simpering voice replete with upper class accent never did convey authority, he knew how to get her attention and guarantee her help. "Zinka's and Pino's favors can be yours."

The hammer dropped to the floor, her mouth hung open. Here was someone who raised the bar for oral fixation. Neither gender nor dignity — nothing — got in the way. Bertie, not inured to such things himself, deeply admired her.

"Maybe they weren't formally sextons, but that's what we call them," Sophia said, trying to be accommodating so as to get the promised reward. "They were the caretakers of the churches, at least, the ones who pressed the vestments and polished the chalices during all of those years when there were no priests. During those communist years when all that was allowed was to say the rosary and pray the novena to the Infant of Prague."

Bertie sat on the coffin next to Sophia. He remembered something in one of his counseling classes about remaining at eye-level with someone who is in a weaker position. Which is the reason priests and nurses squat down to speak with a woman in a wheelchair rather than standing over her. It just makes them more relaxed. Not that any of this mattered to Sophia who was staring intently at Pino's bulging crotch, the only comfort she truly longed for. This reward in mind, Sophia needed no further prompting.

"These men, because they were all men, were the caretakers of the 'treasures of Bohemia,' as the High Priestess calls them. Splendid chasubles, elaborate altar dressings and paintings, glorious paintings. Those are her words too, I've heard here speak of them so often, as did her husband before her. They say that if they were French or German from the same period they would be priceless. But so far there is no such interest in our art. But since we are entering the European Community, since Prague has been discovered by the outside world, that will change." Sophia looked longingly at Pino and then at Bertie, hoping that she had told them all they wanted or at least enough.

"I need to know one thing more." Bertie interjected, realizing that for Pino any information and anytime was just fine. "It's about the man we saw when we were behind the arras together." Sophia was expressionless, as if she didn't remember or chose not to remember who it was that Bertie was talking about. "The one you called the Pontifex Maximus."

"Oh him," Sophia said, tossing the question off lightly. "I just thought he might be the Pontifex Maximus because he looked pretty distinguished and I haven't seen, none of us have ever seen, the Pontifex Maximus."

"Was it or wasn't it?" Bertie tried to pin her down.

"Could have been, I really don't know," was all Sophia could say.

"Find out for me," Bertie said in his firmest of tones. Even though he had no doubt about Otger being behind this whole, nefarious operation, he knew that Brocard would need proof and wanted to be armed with it whenever it was needed. "Find out where he is in the castle and what he is up to."

As Sophia nodded her consent, Bertie nodded his to Pino who began unzipping his trousers and slowly, ever so slowly as he was such a pro at this, pulled out his cock.

"By the way, what are you going to do with this?" Bertie pointed to the coffin they were getting up from, she to kneel in front of Pino and him to watch from the corner.

"The mud will cover it up." Then realizing an explanation might be needed, Sophia added, "I'll just knock a hole in the wall with that pick over there and the mud will come oozing in. Cozier than six feet under."

Fraught with danger as this was, it was no more bizarre than standing in the corner watching the man he loved being blown by some lowlife—and a woman at that.

37

Brocard refused to believe it could be as simple as that. What is, after all, especially in matters of spirituality? According to Judy's theory, Quietism simply collapsed under its own weight. This whole monumental movement of self-knowledge, of enlightenment laced with lunacy, with Madame Guyon at its head, simply imploded. But he knew that external forces came into play. That church politics and abuses of power had much to do with the demise of these mystics. Just as he knew that there were forces bearing down on Zinka and her sister's ill begotten Church.

Suddenly he realized that the two mysteries paralleled each other, were caught up one in another. He knew that in solving one, the other would be solved. If there were such a thing as celibate's intuition, this would have to be the stellar example. But how was he to prove it? And more to the point, which he meant to solve first: the driving force behind Madame Guyon that threatened to bring down the church or the power behind the High Priestess that was wreaking havoc and death in Bohemia?

Brocard had never lost that deeply religious, decidedly comforting sense that an unseen force, an omniscient power had a unique plan for him. Free will only went so far, in his mind. The great arc of his life, the craziness from cradle to grave had purpose. And was, ultimately, out of our hands. If this was true for him — and he had no doubt it was, must it not hold true for Zinka, Judy and Madame Guyon? In God's eye it all made sense, of this he had no doubt. What was uncertain was how, not if, he would understand why. Because, tenacious little monk that he was, he would get to the bottom of it. He must.

Events were beginning to move fast. In a few hours Brocard would be on a plane to Holland, where he was to stop for a couple of days on his way to Prague. Although there was no opportunity right now to conjure up Madame Guyon's world, something necessary to answer some key questions, there surely would be after he had landed in Europe. More to the point, Avertanus had promised to give Brocard the mystical tomes that would enable him to access the past and even the future. This was no less than the *Conclusiones Magicae*, a sixteenth century copy of which Avertanus had guarded for as long as anyone had known him. In fact, this arcane text had been the very focus of Avertanus's intellectual and spiritual life. Many's the night Brocard could remember the old scholar pouring over it in his carol in the library at the Monastery of San Redempto, obsessively poring over every word, making annotations in the margins in that cramped script of his. A chill went through Brocard's body as he realized that there could be one reason and one reason only that Avertanus was prepared to now share these spells and incantations. He must know that he is dying and was going to entrust them to Brocard. As both mentee and friend, Brocard knew that this must be the case. Honoured as he was, losing Avertanus was something he was not prepared to do just yet. Then again, there was such a strong, deeply spiritual bond that he never would be prepared to lose him.

One obligation remained before he had to leave. Brocard had promised Judy that he would attend a talk she was giving at the local meeting of The Voice of the Faithful. Although it wasn't officially sanctioned — or maybe because of that, rebel that he was, Brocard quietly admired the good work this group was doing. He would go on their website occasionally to see what they were up to; he followed their growth from a small group of Boston Catholics, outraged by the sex scandals that rocked the church, to the thousands of local chapters inserted in dioceses nationally, that called for accountability. Judy having been asked to present a paper at the chapter that met at Mount Olivet Academy for Women gave him a wonderful opportunity to support her, while seeing first hand the group he had read so much about. The timing could have been better, of course, but years of religious life had made Brocard rather used to awkward timing, to schedules that were not of his own choosing. And, with that faith that all things are for a purpose, he made his way across campus to the meeting. Knowing that, at the very least, it would boost Judy's confidence to see her advisor there.

Brocard knew that there was no danger that he would miss his flight. His bags had long-since been packed and the taxi would be there to pick him up with hours to spare. Ever compulsive, Brocard had to get to every appointment early out of fear of being late for anything. But there was no danger of that this afternoon, even if Judy rambled on.

The Music Room in the Administration Building was where the Voice of the Faithful Meeting was being held. A small lounge, just right for the twenty or so participants. It was large enough for them not to feel cramped and small enough so that they did not have to raise their voices — for they were, he noticed immediately, a soft-spoken, almost sheepish group. Despite the furor they had caused in the church, despite the ban on their meetings and harsh pronouncements about them from several key bishops, Brocard was taken aback to see how restrained and well-behaved these men and women were. Interestingly, they were divided down the middle by gender, yet rarely seemed to be couples. A well-heeled, well-dressed gathering. Brocard could not help but wonder if some of the money they saved by holding it from the collection plate at church had ended up on their backs. If so, he thought, it was money tastily well spent.

A dowager opened the meeting with that mandatory gravitas that all dowagers have. After a few business items, and an equally brief recognition of Father Brocard's presence, she introduced Judy McCabe, "a bright young woman who is doing some interesting research on one of the first true lay movements of spirituality, Quietism."

Brocard was impressed at how professional, even mature Judy looked. Her hair was pulled back rather severely from her face; she had abandoned the co-ed jeans for a dark gray pantsuit with a plunging bodice. An unexpected touch that worked.

But the hint of flesh was not all that was to take Brocard by surprise. Just as he was settling in for a regurgitation of her research project, the unexpected happened. A flash of genius? Originality? Call it what you will, it caught him completely off-guard.

"I will not patronize you by telling you things you already know, laced in the language of academia that I have been learning how to use." She caught Brocard's eye and gave him a little smile of recognition then sped on, with a series of associations that were dazzling. "Quietism was the first truly modern spirituality as it not only threatened the very purpose of the organized church—by abolishing the need for priestly given sacraments—but," and here she paused for dramatic impact, "by being the first truly lay movement."

Brocard could have objected, of course. The *Devotio Moderna* two centuries before had a better claim to this. But Judy was so fired up, so convincing, and obviously going somewhere fast, that interrupting her was not an option.

"No, what I want to tell you about is a specific meeting which I think is applicable to you at this time. To the laity in the church, trying to give voice to a new spirituality in the face of a hierarchy that will do anything in its power to silence it.

"The meeting I am referring to took place in March of 1695. Fénelon, that great friend and supporter of Madame Guyon, was asked to put his signature to the Thirty Four Articles worked out by the Commission of Issy."

Ever so briefly, displaying a facility for synopsis that

Brocard had not thought her capable of, Judy explained what these Articles spelt out—how they were meant to limit the nature and practise of Quiet Prayer, in subtle yet profound ways. The end game, of course, was complete and total allegiance to the Church. But it was not what but *who* was behind it, that shook Brocard out of his stupor and finally made him see the light.

"The rivalry between Fénelon and Bishop Bossuet, his superior, is perhaps the most famous in all of the history of Christian Spirituality. Traditionally, it has been thought that Bossuet acted out of jealousy. Or that, he was at best a ploy of conservative elements in the church.

"What I have discovered, and have the documentation to back up, is that Bossuet was the major player in this. That he in fact goaded Fénelon on, that he was forever advancing his own agenda. And that agenda was clear: the more he could diminish the power of Madame Guyon and her followers, diminish the power of the laity that were following her in increasing numbers, the more he enlarged his own power base.

"It was Bossuet who encouraged Madame Guyon and Fénelon to write down their thoughts. His taunting drew them out of the bushes where they had taken cover, making them easy prey. Bossuet, that smarmy little bishop, prejudiced the mind of King Louis—Bossuet was, after all, the tutor of the Dauphin and had unparalleled access to the king. He was, quite simply, behind it all. A puppeteer nimbly making characters come and go, dance and sit. For one reason only: power."

Brocard sat immobile in his seat.

"Bossuet. Of course it must be him." Suddenly everything made sense.

38

*F*ood had simply never been one of her passions, which was somewhat of a disgrace given the fact that she was French to the core. Actually, for that matter, she had no passions, a characteristic or lack thereof that isolated Camille even more. This was not to say that what she felt for Zinka was not love—love it was, but in her own, rather lifeless, practical and analytic way. The world does march by in twos, as her mother had always assured her. It is just easier to have a companion. And, if a woman is constructed to love another woman, why not opt for quantity? It only made sense, after all.

What was getting tiresome for Camille, was the Herculean effort necessary to sustain this relationship she had chosen: the lies that had to be told not to mention the games that had to be played. Not with Zinka directly as things turned out. Jealousy had become the least of her problems. In fact, her little contretemps with Pino, as unpleasant as such things are for her, seemed to have put a rest to all of those feelings. It was empowering for Camille to know that she could fight back in kind; could cause jealousy as well as feel it. No, what was tiresome was the way she increasingly had to come to Zinka's rescue, get her out of jams she had no right getting into in the first place.

And now she was being forced to meet over food with Dr. Emil Rothenberg, to have to spend time with that obese bore as he stuffed his mouth with boiled cabbage and seared beef. All because this was what had to be done to get to the bottom of the mess that Zinka had gotten herself into with Natalia. It was all too terribly, terribly tiresome.

"*Par ici*," Emil called out as he saw Camille enter the restaurant where they had arranged to meet. "*Ici*," he mumbled again, waving the fingers of one hand lethargically in front of him. It was too much of an effort for Emil to raise himself out of the chair and, besides, as Camille was fashionably late, he had already ordered some lovely appetisers that it was impossible for him to abandon for even a moment, tasty as they were.

"My dear Mademoiselle," he said reaching for her hand, then rubbing his greasy mouth over it as if he were considering ingesting her. "You are too kind to accommodate me by coming to Prague."

"*Franchement*," Camille said as she took a seat across the table from Emil so as to preclude the possibility of sharing a banquette with him, "it was not easy to leave the commune. They are very attentive about the comings and, particularly, the goings of their initiates, which is as I told you what I have become out of necessity. But they believed my story about having family business to settle." Emil had put down his fork just long enough to give Camille a look that she found decidedly unsettling. Could it be lust?

"Your cheekbones give your face such a beautiful line. And who ever would believe that lips could be as thin and, how shall I say, transparent as yours are?"

Choosing not to respond, for fear of leading him on into territory that she for one had no stomach for, she signalled the waiter nearest their table. Just a simple salad, anything, with the dressing on the side of course, she ordered in an authoritative tone. Then, she questioned Emil as to why he had declined her invitation to visit the Castle of the Church of Doom, as she had arranged. It was her hope, she told him, that in seeing what they were up against, he might better assist her free Zinka from the snare she was in.

"My dear mademoiselle," Dr. Rothenberg burped out as he reached for another fried something, "I am simply not made of the same metal as you—I have no stomach, if you will excuse the turn of speech, for danger. Intrigue, yes, what Frenchman does not long for that after all? And art always. But even the faintest suspicion of bodily harm (and, mademoiselle, you have mentioned that the Castle is virtually strewn with corpses) makes me run, or at least move myself as best I can, in the opposite direction."

"Strewn with corpses is a bit of an exaggeration. There are only three, possibly four that we have discovered."

"For me, timid creature that I am mademoiselle, that is an army of death and decay." Partially masticated globs of food clung to Emil's smiling mouth. "Besides, where I believe I can be most helpful, is in identifying and evaluating the artworks you have mentioned. I am," he added "perhaps the world's expert on Bohemian Baroque."

This information came as a shock to Camille. Perhaps Zinka knew this, but as Zinka was a lost cause, the one who had to be rescued after all, she could not be counted on to help. Camille was sure that Bertie, who had taken the lead in solving this case, was not familiar with this either. And why she wondered, had it taken Dr. Rothenberg so long to tell her this? All she knew was that he had an interest in the period. The fact that, if he was telling the truth, Emil knew better than anyone else not only what these paintings and objects were but probably where and to whom they could be sold. Art historians, Zinka had proven so well, had long since ceased to be pure academics, being major players in the making and breaking of art markets.

"My dear mademoiselle," Emil started. Being referred to as a mademoiselle—an unmarried girl—was beginning to infuriate Camille. At her age, she was Madam, married or not. Then again, everything about Dr. Emil Rothenberg turned her delicate stomach, from his eating with his mouth open to his morbid obesity. She decided to hear him out and make as rapid an exit as possible. "Bohemian art will assuredly be financially lucrative— massively so, in my opinion. Although the market may be undeveloped now, the quality is there, not to mention the scarcity of truly great works, to assure the fact that major prices will be paid for these items in the not too distant future."

"And are any of the works I mentioned 'major?'" Camille asked, sensing that he might indeed be playing with her.

Emil finished the last morsel on his plate, laid down his utensils and gave her a long and meaningful stare. "*Peut-être,* mademoiselle," he muttered, "perhaps. You let me know, won't you, if you discover anything of interest. I plan to spend a week, maybe more in this glorious city where one eats so well."

His words were so unctuous, so ingenuous that she knew in an instant that he was, indeed, hiding something. What exactly, she could not say. But as surely as she found Dr. Emil Rothenberg perverse and disgusting, she now knew him to be untrustworthy as well. Why would he have made the trip out to Prague to meet her if he were not going to cooperate?

Camille La Blanchierderie, proper French matron that she was, now felt herself to be the orphan. The world around her appeared as what it was, a hostile place where there was often little comfort to be had. Without family, lover, friends to rely on, Camille was feeling very much alone. She thanked Dr. Rothenberg for his help and assured him she would call him should anything develop. Then she gathered herself together and, under his licentious gaze, made her way out into the night and back to the Castle of the Age of Doom.

39

*T*f you can't tell your own sister that you have had a sex change, well then, who on earth can you tell? That, at least, was Zinka's thinking as she made the decision to reveal her true identity to the High Priestess Natalia, her long lost sister.

Needless to say Zinka had given the matter some thought. Not a great deal of thought, mind, as she was of an impulsive nature. But, quite a bit, all things considered.

Not surprisingly perhaps, given the dramatic flair she brought to everything, location was her major concern. For Zinka, food tasted better and sex was far more pleasurable, if the location was just right. This same logic applied for those critical, truth-sharing moments in life which all of us must endure. Of course, such moments did not factor too largely into Zinka's life, as she always felt that truth was highly over-rated. Still, the time had arrived to come clean with Natalia; and the place she had chosen for this thunderous revelation was splendid.

In her wanders throughout the Castle, Zinka had stumbled across a beautifully proportioned room in the West Turret. It was a bit too sparsely furnished for her taste—just a writing desk and an oversized wingback chair—but otherwise had much to recommend it. First, it was off the beaten track. There was no possibility of their being rudely interrupted. Second, it was perfectly circular, ideal for constant motion, for keeping the person you are talking to off guard. And finally, it had majesty. The ceiling height exalted but didn't intimidate; there were remnants of a mythological fresco on the walls to give gravitas; and, more important still, only one door out, so that Zinka could make that all-important gesture of blocking egress, should Natalia want to bolt. Perfect.

After the location had been chosen, the next decision that had to be made was what to wear. Zinka had, as has been said before, the unforgiving intensity of a convert. Nothing whatsoever could be taken for granted in this grand, new world of femininity. The hair, the nails, the color of her ensemble—which everything she wore always was, as everything went together—all was calculated to a fault. Right down to her undergarments, the panties and stockings, with garters or without, bras or halter tops. Actually, especially her undergarments would be more to the point, as she invariably found herself disrobing.

She decided on a dark green Tartan skirt with a cream-colored blouse, blouson and décolleté, of course, to highlight her greatest asset. Despite the hardship of trudging up the worn turret staircase in heels, she had decided on toeless stilettos of Nile Crocodile. There was nothing quite like the buzz she got when sporting endangered species. And as for the hair, what the hell, she had radically pulled it back from her face and attached the ponytail fall. Sure it made her look like a cheerleader, but with legs and tits like hers, what could be wrong with a little cheering? And the face, after all, was what she shared with Milorad, her former self. Give or take a little makeup.

The sun was setting as Zinka prowled around the room waiting for Natalia to arrive. She did so hope that her sister, how she longed to call her that, would not be late as the light that flooded the room was the most flattering of the day. If she missed it, Zinka thought as she moved about the room in search of the most fitting place for Natalia to discover her, then she would have to light candles as there was no electricity in this part of the Castle. But she had only brought candles for an emergency, as she never felt they flattered her, lingering, as they did, too much on her firm jaw and large hands.

"This is highly irregular, as I am sure you know, Professoressa." Natalia's first words as she entered the room were not encouraging. "And so are the clothes you are wearing, I might add. You are, or so I had come to believe, an initiate, are you not?"

"I do apologize, your reverence," Zinka cooed, laying on the charm, "but I thought you might enjoy a little change of scenery. And," she continued moving ever so slowly along the wall to keep Natalia off guard, "I thought that getting out of that white schmatta and dressing up like a real girl might please you."

"I haven't been up here since my husband passed over," Natalia mumbled under her breath. She had a habit of zoning out, that sister of hers, and Zinka was not going to allow that to happen.

This was her moment, after all, not some dead man's.

"Give me a kiss, please, I have something to tell you that is not easy." Natalia did not resist at all as Zinka got closer. What immediately became clear to Zinka — how could she have been such a stupid girl she thought — was that her heels were far too high. How on earth was she going to rest her head on Natalia's shoulder, towering over her as she was? realizing that her muscular legs would not fail her, she crouched low as she planted a kiss on Natalia's cheek and then ever so gently placed her head on her sister's shoulder. Fortunately Natalia was staring at her husband's old desk, lost in thoughts that Zinka sincerely hoped she would keep to herself, so she did not see Zinka's rather ludicrous contortion.

"Natalia my dear, I am your long lost brother Milorad."

"Yes, I thought somehow you might be," was all she had to say. Then she added in a voice more reminiscent of a lost girl than a High Priestess, "stay with me, will you?"

"Always." Zinka said holding her. This was not the first time in her life that she realized that those revelations that we think of as most difficult are really quite simple.

40

"*A*nd what exactly does that mean, might I ask?" It was clear that Camille's nerves were on edge but, this was Camille after all, and even she was surprised at such an outburst. "Explain yourself," she continued shaking, unable to maintain control.

"I was just trying to say," Pino stammered, "that Zinka asked me to help her choose the outfit she was going to wear for an important meeting with the High Priestess, and we made sure she put on the loose panties — the lace ones that slip down so easily," he added hastily as if that explained everything.

"Has absolutely everyone had sex with my girlfriend?" Camille blurted out.

"Well, probably, yes," Pino confirmed, thinking that this was more a badge of honour than anything else. Disgrace, shame, even jealousy were no concepts that computed very well for Pino. He was, after all, a hustler and whores just have their own values.

Even the healer, Bertie offered what he thought were some consoling words. "I do think we're talking on cross-purposes here."

"Oh shut up you English faggot," Camille shouted back at him. For some reason Pino found this funny, terribly funny and could not help but laugh.

"Faggot," he smiled pointing at Bertie, then he blurted out, "English," which he seemed to find equally amusing. Humour, Bertie thought, was a uniquely personal thing.

"Stop it now, stop it both of you." Years of being a priest had taught Bertie well on how to be haughty and assertive when needed. They had work to do after all.

"We are not here to talk about Zinka's panties or my sexual proclivities, so just knock it off, will you?" Both Camille and Pino seemed honestly impressed with Bertie's newfound commanding presence. "Now sit down both of you and answer my question."

Still flushed, Camille took a place on the nearest bench. Pino, perhaps wanting to make amends or just out of force of habit, sat down so close to her that their bodies touched. He moved away quickly however when Camille gave him one of her how-dare-you looks that Parisians do so well. They each looked up at Bertie like bad puppies.

"You first Pino," Bertie started, being careful that his voice didn't slide up into the higher register he was used to speaking in. "Did you make arrangements for Father Brocard's visit?"

Pino nodded yes.

"You made up a false name, I hope?"

"Smith," Pino blurted back.

"Very subtle," Bertie answered, realizing once again that Pino had no strengths outside the bedroom. But thanking God, at least, for that blessing.

"And you," Bertie said turning his attention to Camille. "What was the outcome of your meeting with Dr. Emil Rothenberg? Did he confirm our suspicions about Otger?"

"Disgusting and unsettling." Camille shook with rage, unable to control the emotions that were welling within her. "I find it hard to imagine that sensibilities so refined are housed in so coarse and objectionable a body."

"This is not about fat people here, Camille," Bertie said looking down on her emaciated body, "this is about stolen art and death and solving the mystery before there is more of both. So please let us just keep to the point here."

"The point is," Camille said standing up to face Bertie, "Emil Rothenberg is one of the world's experts on Bohemian Baroque art. The point is, he knows more than we think and that Otger, your precious little Otger, may very well not be in this alone."

Camille was no one's idiot. If they thought her a worm, well watch her turn.

41

*T*he smell of death was beginning to get to her. Wherever she went in the Castle she remembered another body she had discovered dead, another corpse she had buried. How many it had been, Sophia no longer knew. Six, maybe seven, she no longer knew. It no longer mattered. Each had their own look, their own weight, their own smell.

Initially it was simply a task that she performed, a privileged task at that as it had brought her into contact with the High Priestess Natalia and now, the Pontifex Maximus himself. She had heard the High Priestess call Otger this herself and had no doubt that Bertie's suspicions were right. This indeed was the man who held the ultimate power, the knowledge of not only what had happened but of what would be happening.

Despite all of the disparaging words she had heard Pino and Bertie say about the Church, and despite what she had seen with her own eyes, her belief in the Church was unshaken. Others might see the hoarding of wealth and the exploitation of the weak, but such was Sophia's faith, that she was able to see through these weaknesses to the deeper truth, that was not venal; the source of power that was not natural at all, but supernatural. This knowledge was, to her, the greatest gift; to others, of course, her sad delusion.

What threatened her resolve and shattered her inner peace was the conviction that the building that housed the Church was dying. Even though she had known that the Church itself was more than stone and mortar, that it was above all those who held authority, the wisdom they had and the assurance they gave, Sophia had heard its cry and knew, as surely as she did with a human death rattle, that its end had come.

The groaning of the very walls would not stop. She knew that others did not hear things as well as she did — 'Sophia and the dogs hear first' was what the villagers used to say, and they were right. She heard a train in the distance by standing upright and being attentive, without listening to the tracks the way the other kids had to do. And minutes before the tremors shook her village, she woke her parents and brothers with her cries, knowing that danger was coming. Warning them.

Was there no one to listen to her now? No one who cared to save themselves? Perhaps even if they knew, they would decide as she herself had to pass beyond with the building itself, like one great caravan to the stars. Still, should she not warn them?

The groaning in her ears and the pestilence of the air slowed her every move. The Pontifex Maximus at least should know what she did. It was her responsibility to tell him alone, then he could decide what to do with this information. Perhaps he would decide that it is better no one knows, perhaps to tell the community of the impending doom. But this was not her decision to make but his.

Mud was oozing out from under the doors on her right as she made her way down the central corridor of the second floor. How long would it take for the buckling doors to burst and for the weight of the second floor to collapse through to the ground floor. The community was gathering for worship in the great chamber below. Were they to be entombed under a mountain of mud? Or was her mind, perhaps, playing tricks with her? Was she not getting carried away, as her mother often told her. Poor Sophia, she would say lovingly stroking her child's hair, such an excitable creature. Unless she finds a man to protect her from life, whose to say what will become of her?

Sophia knew where to find Otger, there was only one place he could be. The Treasury, as he called it, had been his virtual home for the past few days. As she had not seen him eat or sleep, she seriously wondered if he was not beyond such human needs. All she had seen him do was to study the notes that Professoressa Zinka had written, inspect the trove of paintings and objects and make more notes himself. Sophia knew too that there had been a great deal of coming and going these past couple of days. The Treasury door opened onto a hastily constructed loading dock and as quickly as the Ponitfex Maximus could prepare things to go, onto a waiting truck they went. To where, she did not know nor care to, as this was not information that she needed to have. Faith, in him and the mission of the Church, sufficed.

It is hard to describe the groaning that Sophia heard, the plaintive moan that was beginning to drive her to distraction. It was deeper than the mooing of a cow, more distressing than the muted braying of a donkey in danger, knowing all is lost.

Sophia was holding her ears when she finally found Otger in the far corner of the Treasury. He was so preoccupied with what he was doing that he did not look up.

"Remarkably beautiful, aren't they?" he asked her, expecting no answer. "They are a series of Lactating Madonnas by Briedl, using the classic icon trope."

Of course Sophia did not hear a word that he said, her ears stopped up as they were. But even if they weren't she wouldn't have understood anything. Otger was used to talking to himself, surrounded by cretins as he was.

"I am here to tell you something very important, Pontifex Maximus," Sophia began, anxious to get her information out before it was too late.

"Stop calling me that stupid name," Otger shot back. "Your High Priestess is having you on with that, don't you see? It's a joke?"

"Is it a joke that this whole Castle is dying?" Sophia yelled back over the groaning of the walls and the pounding in her head. He laughed at her. She knew that to him it was.

42

"Yes indeed it is I, Father Bertram. So good to hear your voice." Despite his excitement at hearing his old friend's voice, Brocard could not get over his formality. He was Roman trained, after all.

"Call me Bertie, please, Father Brocard. Did you have a pleasant journey?" Bertie, at least, had overcome his problems with familiarity.

"The interminable security checks and waits at the airport plus the flight gave me a good opportunity to think," Brocard told his old friend. "And what I have decided, if you don't think me too rash to offer, is that this whole situation at the Church of Doom might be far more complicated than any of us have imagined."

The old pedant, Bertie thought. Everything about Brocard's words, the tone of his voice, even his studied pauses, reminded Bertie of the way Brocard's boring rambling style, slowed to a halt every house chapter in Rome. These were meant to be practical meets, about finances and the day to day operation of the monastery and instead, Father Brocard would get on his high horse and waffle on about his feelings or underlying philosophy or God-knows-what. No, Bertie had figured this out. He and Pino were on the scene, working daily with the clues, after all. His old nemesis Otger was behind it all, from stolen art to corpses, and Brocard's musings were not going to dissuade him of this.

"Granted there is something neat and clean about it being Otger," Brocard continued undeterred. "But life is messier than that, don't you see? Even in novels, good ones at least, tidy little endings are suspect. Then again," Brocard said not coming up for air, "might this evil not resist solving? Might it not be a dark Thanatopsis, flowering unseen and unappreciated, destined to die out before it is ever fully know?"

Now Brocard had gone too far. There were murders to solve and art to recover and Bertie for one was going to see that the task got done. Wasn't it bad enough that Brocard's partner, Zinka — because everyone saw them that way, except perhaps the couple themselves — had been blinded to her task by incestuous lust? It was not that Bertie was getting moralistic, of course — an ex-priest shacked up with a hustler can hardly take the high road. But rather frustrated that he had to go it alone, with obstructions now from a dithering monk.

"Do you have a pen?" Bertie asked Brocard, all but shouting into the phone.

"Yes, I do," Brocard replied. "And you needn't speak so loud, Father Bertram, the connection is quite good really and my hearing, thank God, is fine."

"Here are the directions to get out here from Prague," Bertie said lowering his voice but keeping the same intensity and he told Brocard what train to take and what to tell the taxi. "Your papers will be here under the assumed name of John Smith."

"Very original," Brocard quipped. "And whose brilliant idea was that one?"

"Pino's if you must know." Bertie was all set to defend his lover, dumb as he might be, but it never came to that. "Well we are in Bohemia, after all," Brocard mused, "so John Smith just might be the most uniquely uncommon name."

When Bertie hung up, Brocard realized that he was shaking, physically shaking. Their conversation, Bertie's dismissive manner above all, triggered memories about their years together in Rome that, until that moment, Brocard had successfully buried. Bertie had been a student of his when he first entered the Order over thirty years ago. Even with the zeal of a novice and the blush of piety, Bertie's impetuous nature was evident. And how could Brocard forget the way Bertie flaunted his relationships, taunting the more conservative members of the community like Brocard and his mentor Avertanus, with his radical ideas and practises. He was a good-hearted soul, Bertie, but unfortunately he used his heart profligately and his body with greater abandon still. To think that

Bertie was leading an investigation and was all but ordering Brocard about was insupportable.

Introvert that he was, the thought of Prague at night held no charm for Brocard. He was, however, intent on hearing from Avertanus, who had promised to email him. So even before unpacking his toiletries bag and lining up the items in orderly fashion on the sink, he plugged in his laptop computer. Ever reliable, Avertanus had not failed him:

My dear Brocard,

My time is short so I will give you the information you requested about the form, invocation and posture necessary to project yourself into Madame Guyon's life. The first thing it is important for you to realizing is that your physical location on the planet is of no consequence. Hers is, I assure you, quite fixed, both in space and time. So all that is needed is for you to enter the door. In other words, you should have no difficulty being with her from your hotel room in Prague.

What is vital is that you center yourself in the same way, since the candle has worked before I would suggest you don't deviate from this devise. However, the incantation will differ, and I have listed two below, taken from the diciplina arcana of spells. Recite the first slowly and reverentially. Should it not work, pause for a good five minutes and proceed to the second, far more powerful incantation. Bon viaggio, my dear friend. In more ways than you can imagine.

Your brother and friend, Avertanus

Ten minutes later, in the midst of the second incantation, Brocard effortlessly entered the door to the seventeenth century for the final time.

43

*P*rison obviously agreed with her. There was a flush to

Madame Guyon's cheeks and a steely resolve in her eyes, which gave her a maturity he had never seen before. Dignified she always was, of course. A lady of her upbringing, not to mention era, unfailingly carried herself well. Just as she could only be well dressed and impeccably groomed. Her maid attended her, of course, in prison. Ostracised and criminal she might be, but this was Paris after all and protocol had to be maintained at all costs.

Because of his frequency and, indeed, facility in being transported into her world, Brocard knew exactly the time and place in which he was. There was no longer any need for him to try and pick up clues to find out what he was witnessing. Nor did anyone have to tell him that he was in Madame Guyon's cell in the Bastille. The year was 1695. That would make Madame Guyon 47 years old. Remarkably young for her age, Brocard thought as he wandered around the sparsely furnished suite of rooms to which she had been confined. One of the many privileges of wealth is the way it slows down the ageing process. It was not surprising that her maid, a good twenty years younger, was the one who appeared the older. Not just menial work but lack of prospects and being told that you are inferior, wear down the body as well as the spirit.

Brocard had become used to being invisible. In fact, he once caught himself laughing about the fact that even as a monk at St. Redempto people often looked through him. He had always been an inconspicuous, some might say inconsequential, type of person. To be invisible even to himself still took him back a bit. What was still a little disconcerting, however, was that he was even invisible to himself in these time travels. Were he to put out his hand in front of him, as he was doing now to run his finger down the margins of the manuscript page on the desk, he saw nothing at all although he knew full well that his hand was there. Curious indeed.

Pedant to a fault, Brocard wondered at the beauty of Madame Guyon's penmanship. Its fluid lines and perfectly balanced proportions belied the fact that this was incendiary material, worthy of condemnation and even excommunication. That, at least, was the party line that he had been taught and, good Catholic that he was, unquestioningly believed. Why else would the Protestants take her on as one of theirs? This turn of events would have shocked, and possibly amused her. Like Luther before her, the desire was to reform the church not break with it. But everyone knows that what we wish for and what we get differ in ways impossible to foresee.

It was not easy for Brocard to concentrate on the text she had written with all of the confusion swirling around him. They were preparing for a visit from someone important, that much he could tell. The maid, high strung at best of times, was fluttering around the room and Madame Guyon, making sure everything was in order—fluffing the cushion on the bed, arranging the armchair so that it commanded the corner of the cell and checking that Madame's shawl hung properly down her back. The mystic herself seemed composed but apprehensive, as she waited, arms folded at her front, for the visit.

How Brocard wanted to simply sit at the desk and read the original text of one of Madame Guyon's works. He knew even before Judy's thesis had come to him, that she was a prolific writer, having written volumes of works on scripture and spirituality. Intriguingly, she seems to have written these in trances, with absolutely no research and, if truth be known, little formal education. She maintained that her works were 'given to her by God.' She, Madame Guyon, was merely a scribe taking his dictation. Channeling is what Shirley MacLaine and her lot would call it in the twentieth century. But over three hundred years earlier, there were no words for this. There were, however, powerful church censors, Inquisitional in nature if not name, who saw this process as far more demonic than divine. This alone, regardless of content, was enough to land her in jail.

The words on the page flowed as beautifully as the script in which they had been written. Highly repetitive, almost poetic, she wrote about 'Passive Love' that consumed her very being, 'annihilating' who she was until God alone, the Spouse, resided within and they were no longer two but one. If he had not known these words were Madame Guyon's, he might have thought they were St. Teresa of Avila's, that great Christian Mystic and Doctor of the Church. There was, of course, something missing in Guyon's writing. Call it what you will—deference, obsequiousness or caution—St. Teresa always assured the reader that she was a mere woman, that she was unschooled, that she might be in error and prayed to God she wasn't. Brocard couldn't find a hint of that tone in the pages before him. In fact, her assurance was complete, her defiance of the ignorant total. This, he grasped in an instant, was her true sin. Women rarely had expressed themselves this way before. Nor could they still write in such a tone without inviting authority's wrath.

Brocard's musings were shattered by the arrival of the dignitary they had been waiting for. When the door swung open, the maid dropped to a profound curtsey. Madame Guyon, affecting a welcoming smile, froze in her place, her hand extended to be kissed by reflex.

His Excellence Bishop Bossuet, resplendent in crimson and lace, glided over to her with an effortlessness that belied his girth. Brocard smiled as he recalled referring to poofy fat boys like this as "big girls." Big girl he was, this powerful bishop who was Bishop Fénelon's nemesis — and, in turn, of Madame Guyon herself.

"I trust you find your surroundings comfortable, Madame?" Although Bossuet's face was placid, there was a sneer in his voice that revealed just how contemptuous he was of her.

"We reside," Madame said using the royal we, "comfortably within, Monsignor. Exterior objects are of little concern. Mere things cannot touch the Ground of our being."

"Yes, yes," Bossuet said dismissively as he made his way to the one armchair in the room and sat down. Better for the woman to stand, he thought to himself, and learn her place. It might help as well to put her off-guard, unsettle her somewhat, although the possibility of this — given her extreme arrogance and lack of respect for authority — seemed pretty remote. It took several minutes for the corpulent bishop to arrange himself in the chair. Mercifully he had the assistance of the young cleric who attended him, the scribe who doubled as valet at times like this. After the folds of his cassock were put in place and the lace at his hands and neck ruffled out, he signalled for the scribe to go over to the writing table and prepare to memorialise the conversation that was about to take place. As this was standard procedure in ecclesial hearings, frequent occurrences in Madame Guyon's life for many years, she thought nothing of it.

Brocard moved over to the far side of the room so that he could see both of the major players, as it was clear that non-verbals would be as important as the words they spoke. There was no need for him to remind himself that these were two French aristocrats. As such the social rules in which they were well schooled were highly developed.

"Allow me, monsignor," Madame Guyon began with a slight nod of her head, "to congratulate you on having been named the tutor of the Dauphin."

"It is, madame, a great honour." Then, so that the young troublemaker knew to whom she was speaking, "one of many honours his Majesty, the King, has graciously bestowed on me."

"Is my dear friend Monsignor still retained as a Royal tutor?" She asked rather maliciously, looking away from Bossuet as she did so. "In my present circumstances I have not been privy to Court news and only hope he continues to devote his considerable talents for the Royal good."

"Your 'dear friend', as you put it Madam, is still the tutor of the grandson of his Majesty Louis XIV. His appointment, far lower in rank it must be said from mine, is being reconsidered in light of the recent ruling from Rome." Bossuet's tone was as icy as his look was menacing.

Madame Guyon said nothing as her eyes locked Bossuet's. But Brocard could see her shoulders being pulled back and the slight trembling of her hands that she disguised quite well by running them gently over the front of her gown. It was clear to Brocard and perhaps to Bossuet as well, that this news had caught her by surprise.

"This then is the reason for your visit? A decision from Rome?" Her tone was quiet yet firm. It was clear that she was regaining her composure. Or, at the very least, girding herself for the worst — improbable as that might be.

Another part of the mystery of Brocard's entry into Madame Guyon's trials was that he could hear her thoughts as clearly as her words and actions. Every part of her being was transparent to him, almost as if he were seeing himself, fully and completely. Something which, in itself, would be remarkable enough because, as we all know, we so often hide ourselves better to ourselves than to those around us.

Brocard heard Madame Guyon crying out loud to herself,

How could this be? My dear Fénelon, my brilliant disciple, is supported by the Jesuits. How could it be that Innocent XII, the Pope, would disobey the will of the Black Pope, the General of the Jesuit Order? And if he has taken a stand against the truth of my words, will the Pope not have to take one against Teresa of Avila—who everyone knows is a pale shadow of me?

"Your musings, Madame, and those of your associate Fénelon have done great damage to Holy Mother Church, to the True Faith. Your ramblings, Madame, are invariably glib and eccentric, and, if you must know, lacking in all originality. All that talk about the states of infancy, that of apostolate, of death, of burial, of resurrection—badly digested, common coin, Madame. Where you and your friend, as you call him, go too far is with your pronouncements on the state of 'deification.' By the grace of God, through the wisdom of the Church, the extent of the damage you have done and its remedy are now finally being addressed."

Madame Guyon went over to the desk and picked up the papers on which she had been working, that had carefully been laid aside by the scribe. Slowly she began to read from her own writing, walking in Bossuet's direction as she did.

"This passive state of contemplation to which the soul is called by the Spouse is one of pure love. When it is present, there is no longer a difference between the Creator and the Created for they are one. There is nothing that can be done, because all is now possible."

She held out the paper she had read from and, glaring down at the seated Bishop, demanded that he make an account of himself. "Do you or any of your minions deny the truth of what we have written?"

Clearly shaken by her audacity, Bossuet's face reddened in rage. "Madame," he said in a tone bordering on the magisterial, "who do you and your lackey Fénelon think you are?"

"Hear me well, Monsignor, hear me well and understand what I am telling you. You must never, never speak disparagingly of Père Fénelon, because He is my well-beloved son, in whom I am well pleased."

"Blasphemy!" Bossuet shouted. He would have risen to his

feet had he been in better shape. But fat people do not have the option of rapid moves. Still, from the look on his face, Brocard could tell that he had triumphed. "Take that down. Did you get it," he shouted to the scribe. "Record how this woman has used God's very words as if they came from her mouth."

"Yes," Madame Guyon said, turning on the beleaguered scribe, "do make sure you get every one of our words. We have been Deified by the Love of God and transformed into the mouthpiece of God. Take down every word, so that this little man," she said turning on Bossuet, "and history know that I am who I am. That my Will and the Will of the Father are one."

Brocard watched as everyone in the room rearranged themselves, every move choreographed by the protocol of their time. The maid scurried over and dropped to her knees, busying herself with the hem of Madame's gown that had slightly hiked during her outburst. Guyon herself turned her back on the Bishop as a sign of her disdain. Bossuet slowly rose from his chair, signalling the scribe with a flick of his finger, that what he was about to say was not to be recorded. A veritable dumb show, Brocard thought, fraught with meaning.

"It is not enough, Madame, that I inform you that the Pontifex Maximus Innocent XII has condemned the work of your protégé Fénelon. This was the reason for my coming but there is more, far more to tell. It is not enough to tell you that Fénelon's ill-advised work, *The Maximes of the Saints*, has been found in error. It was at your urgings, I have no doubt, that he foolishly associated your delusional states with the greatness of St. Teresa of Avila."

The bishop placed his hand on her back and pushed her abruptly as he said, "turn, Madame, turn and look at me as I tell you what you, in your ignorance have not known."

Madame Guyon did not move instantly, but, after a moment, slowly began to turn towards him. Her maid, attentive to a fault, remained at her feet to assure that Madame's gown fell in proper fashion. Satin did so have a way of riding up the hoop.

"Why was it, do you think Madame, that I began to flush Fénelon's beliefs out by writing pamphlets that forced him to exchange views with me in the public forum? Why was it, have you considered Madame, that I goaded him on so, challenging him in print to defend your rambling delusions? Why was it, do you think Madame, that I was unrelenting in my attack of a spirituality that could so easily be construed as subversive to the Authority of the Pontiff?"

Brocard read Madame Guyon's mind and knew that a woman of her breeding would hold her tongue rather than utter one word of what she was thinking.

"It was I, Madame, His Excellency the Bishop Bossuet, who has played you like a fiddle. It was I, Madam, who knew how to use your delusions and those of your hapless cleric lackeys, to ultimate advantage."

Madame Guyon's response to this news shocked Bossuet as much as it did Brocard. She smiled, broadly and assuredly she smiled.

"Have you no shame, Madame, for having led so many astray? That suicide Père Lacombe, to name one of many, Madame. Have you no shame?"

Madame's face seemed radiant as her smile broadened. Finally, with coldness in her voice, she asked, "What was it, Monsignor, you meant to gain by this?"

Lowering his voice, so that the heavens themselves could not hear, he whispered in her ear. "You were used, Madame. You were a small but important part in a struggle that I have finally won—a struggle to wrest power from the Jesuits, whom the King abhorred and needed to bring down and to assure that the sacramental church, the hierarchy of which I am part, retains total power. You and your lot have served me well, Madame. It is a short way from my position as Bishop to a Cardinalate in the Curia in Rome. My palace is being prepared, Madame, thanks to your ignorant ranting. And your fate, woman, is sealed."

"Is it, Monsignor?" She smiled as if she had not heard or understood a word of what he had said to her. "And what exactly is to be done with me then? Am I to languish in the Bastille?"

Bossuet nodded to the scribe to begin taking notes again.

"No, Madame, I have no intention of making you the martyr you long to be. After a period of time, two to three years no more, paper will be signed for you to be transported to your son's estate in Blois where you are to remain for the rest of your life, never to leave."

"The gardens are lovely at Blois," Madame Guyon commented wryly. The smile on her face enraged Bossuet, but there was nothing he could do about it. Hadn't he won, after all? Didn't Guyon realizing that she had been a pawn in a major power struggle? That her delusions had brought down not only her but also mysticism itself? That by getting the Pope to suppress Fénelon a process had begun that was to mark the demise of the mystics? That from now on passive prayer would be looked on as suspect and personal revelation as dangerous. How Bossuet longed to wipe that smile off her face and bring her crashing down to reality.

"Before you leave, Monsignor, there are some things about the future we would like to let you know. We feel these things are important for you to be aware of so that you are not caught up in pride, that greatest of vices."

The Bishop signalled for his scribe to put away his writing materials and prepare to leave. Then, with the door parted, he turned to Madame Guyon and nodded for her to proceed.

"You will die, Monsignor, then mitre crashing to the ground, grasping vainly for your crosier as you leave this world to go to the judgement awaiting you. I, Monsignor, am to live a long life, dispensing charity to the poor, faithful to the God who deifies me. And rest assured, my poor delusional bishop, mystics cannot be put down, not forever. And women, Monsignor, those women you and your lot feel you are manipulating, will turn your schemes against you."

Church history, that Brocard knew well, confirmed to him that she indeed would outlive them all. However nothing he had ever read had prepared him for Madame Guyon's words, which seemed to speak more to his century than ever they could to hers.

44

*T*he ritual had begun. This time, however, there was to be nothing familiar about it, nothing comforting and surely nothing even remotely sublime. The Great Hall of the Castle of Doom was filled with the remnants of the community, those who had not taken their own lives or not fled into the night fearing the worst. All those present, not just Brocard and his cohorts who were preparing to confront evil, felt the dread looming over them.

The chanting had begun. Were it in Italian, Brocard would have thought it relaxing; but being Slavic, the tone had enveloped him in gloom. As he saw it, many in the room fought off tears and slumped their shoulders like the beaten people that they were. It is safe to say that all who had entered the portal that day had abandoned hope.

The procession had begun. Gone were the dozen initiates, gone too the censor bearer madly wafting clouds of incense in the air. The High Priestess Natalia processed by herself, with her train carried by none other than Zinka. Brocard could control himself not knowing if he should be annoyed that a good Catholic girl should have abandoned herself to such New Age paganism; or whether he should burst out laughing at the sight of Zinka being anyone's slave. Surely, he thought, she can't have fallen for this. But then as the High Priestess Natalia mounted her throne and bared her breasts, he thought better of his having judged Zinka too rashly.

Natalia was quite a girl, he had to admit. Not overly spiritual by his lights, but quite a girl nevertheless. And when Brocard saw Zinka kneel before her and bury her head in her breasts, he finally understood what she saw in her sister and her ersatz-religion. Tits. Pure and simple.

As Natalia began to speak, simple words about 'Pure Love' and finding our 'Inner Goddess', Brocard looked around for Bertie and Pino. Everyone else was there but them. There were the two officers from Interpol off in the right hand corner of the Hall. They had already identified several of the paintings that adorned the walls, stolen from churches all. Fine Baroque canvases of lactating virgins all, just not of the quality they had hoped to find. And long-suffering Camille was also there — eyes riveted to the indiscretions of her girlfriend. Sophia, who was no longer a part of their plans having supplied all of the help they needed, had entered into the ritual as if it were her last—which indeed it was to be: but no Pino or Bertie.

But, knowing what he now did, Brocard was not concerned about their absence. As he saw it, this was not the final but the penultimate chapter. What concerned him more was the mud that was seeping down from the corners of ceiling; what truly troubled him was the way in which the wall behind the throne, the one abutting the mountainside, was buckling and groaning.

It was not only Sophia that heard the Castle's plaintive cry now, it was everyone. And everyone except Zinka and Natalia, who were caught up in their incestuous ritual showed signs of alarm. Yet for some reason none of them moved. Not one. It was not that they were frozen in fear but rather resigned to a fate that was about to consume them whole.

Brocard, of course, would have none of this; nor would Camille who, jealous as she was, longed to resume married life with Zinka who she knew would get over her latest infatuation— as, indeed, she had gotten over many in the past. Nor were the Interpol cops about to sacrifice their lives for some old paintings. A job was a job, after all; life had far greater value.

Suddenly, Bertie burst into the Hall, arms flailing away followed by Pino who was dragging Otger. Brocard put his face in his hands and lamented the day he had ever thought Bertie capable of anything. Bertie, on the contrary, could taste victory and would not be stopped. Panting from the sheer amount of adrenaline coursing through his body, he turned to address the Hall, unaware that the mud had begun to ooze through the surrounding walls.

"My brothers and sisters," he began then checked himself— once a priest always a priest. "Listen up. This whole church is a scam. It's not a church at all, it's a con job. A money making scheme. And this poor woman here," Bertie said pointing to Natalia seated on her throne, "this poor woman has been exploited and used by this despicable man, who calls himself the Pontifex Maximus."

There was a discernible gasp in the Hall that, for one brief moment, drowned out the moan of the building. Could this wretched old man on the ground, the one who had been so unceremoniously dragged in by the attractive Italian stud, could this possibly be the fabled Pontifex Maximus? From the way he was laughing, the answer was probably no.

"Not quite, Father Bertram," Otger said freeing himself from Pino's grasp, standing up and wiping the dust off his trousers with his hands. "You are every bit as impetuous and unobservant as you were at San Redempto, during those many years we were monks together."

Natalia dislodged Zinka's mouth from her breast, the suction was quite something, and rallied to Otger's defense.

"It is true enough I have referred to Professor Otger at times as Pontifex Maximus. But I did so only in jest. It was a little inside joke. He could hardly be the real Pontifex Maximus. The good Professor is only here to help our Church identify, catalogue and appraise the many art works that have been given to us. Nothing more."

Brocard and Interpol knew full well that there was more, but this was not the time to discover it. For no sooner had Natalia finished speaking than the ceiling of the Great Hall buckled and caved in. It all happened in one fluid movement, starting at the center and then working its way inexorably out to the corners. Those who moved quickly saved themselves or had the presence of mind to save others.

Brocard ran up to Bertie, placed his arm around his shoulder and scooted him out of the Hall. Pino, seeing the horror on Camille's face, swept her up in his arms and ran to the nearest door. Zinka, ever the big brother, took Natalia by the hand and eased her gently out. And the two cops ran the hell out of there, not forgetting to rip some paintings off the wall on their way.

For Sophia, the thought of being buried in mud was somehow comforting. How easy the task when nature took over. No coffins to build or dead weight to lift. How efficient she thought as she saw the body parts of other initiates content to meet their fate get buried under the warm earth. Were it not for the panicked screams, it might have been a peaceful moment.

At the side door of the Castle, Zinka gave Natalia a sisterly kiss and bid her goodbye. Theirs had been, needless to say, not the most usual of family reunions. But as Zinka had nothing to compare it with and, being Zinka, always had an expectation of the strange, it suited her fine. Natalia's parting wish was that Zinka not tell anyone that she survived. Zinka, of course, promised her that it would be their little secret and returned Natalia's smile with one which, were her jaw not quite so large and her teeth so many, was almost as radiant.

Brocard separated from Bertie as soon as they were safe outside; as did Camille from Pino. Crisis does make such strange bedfellows. The two Interpol cops, shaken by the experience, nevertheless stayed together. But that after all was their job.

They all took one last look back at the Castle of Doom as they drove away from it. All except Zinka who had the distinct feeling that if she did she would be turned into a pillar of salt.

45

*N*ot much was left to be done. Avertanus had always been an orderly monk; but no time more so than when facing death. Regarding possessions, of course, there was little to do, as he had so few and all of them would resort to the Order on his passing. But in regards to knowledge, the passing on of all he had learnt, it was not so easy. It might have been if Father Dionysius McGreel had continued his studies and become the disciple Avertanus had always hoped he would have. But, as so often happened in religious life, Father's groin got carried away and off Dionysius went to the pear-shaped wife to breed. Avertanus smiled to think how insufferably narrow minded his thinking would seem to many in the world. But he knew better. He knew that if you wanted to push beyond the mundane to accomplish truly great things, you had to abhor the natural and embrace the supernatural. The metaphysical imperative, he called it: the necessity of dedicating oneself totally to the transcendent, so that greatest is reached.

There was no way around it now—only one person to whom he could leave the secrets. Brocard was not the brightest light but he was trustworthy, that at least. Besides which he was caught in the middle of great and cosmic lessons. Without Avertanus around he would need every bit of help he could get to survive the last and final test.

It was late, not only in the night but also in his life, yet there was one final thing he had to do. He had already told Brocard that there was something waiting for him in Zenderen on Brocard's return to America from Prague. And he had also told his prior that the volumes he had spent years researching, that great canon of the Magical Writings (the *Conclusiones Magicae*) with the innumerable annotations, were to be given to Father Brocard when he arrived. All that remained was to write a final letter to accompany this last great gift to his faithful friend.

My dearest friend Brocard,

One of the great lessons that life and study have taught me is that if one knows where to look and how to look there are patterns, discernible patterns to everything. To say that anything is random is to be ignorant of its design. This is as true of mayhem and murder, of crimes and deception, as it is of more noble human enterprises.

In brief, my dear Brocard, I have discerned a pattern to the mysteries that you have been caught up in. It is this: the Elements, my friend. The Four Great Elements. I know I am rushing ahead, but it is for a purpose that I am doing so.

The Mystery of the Poussin paintings, caught up as it was in the apocalyptic flood that brought down the Monastery of San Redempto was water. It purged the evil of that monastery which, in happier times we had both loved so dearly. Secondly, was the Mystery of the Caravaggio, the solving of which involved fire, the conflagration of the prison you ministered in. Now you tell me of the wall of mud bearing down on the site of the ecclesial art theft. I wonder if even now, the destruction by earth has not taken place. Wind, my dear Brocard, wind will await you in your next endeavor — if it hasn't manifested itself as the Spirit of Truth that has blown throughout your trials. Whether it will come and take you with it or propel you into another cycle of activity, another time in which to uncover evil systems and restore justice, I cannot say. What I do know is that you are caught in the midst of a Plan far greater than you can imagine — you and your strange band of sleuths. To what purpose I have not been able to divine. My suspicion is that doing right is purpose enough; that unmasking pretension and showing the lie to those who lord it over others is enough. But finally, what do I know? As Aquinas said before he passed on to his reward, "It's all straw." Straw it is, my dear friend. But how much fun this straw has been.

Your dear friend always,

Avertanus

Having finished all he had to do, Father Avertanus Deblaer, looked out the widow for one last time then lay down on his bed. He said to himself, I feel tired, so very tired, then quietly died. It was an aortal aneurysm that silently burst and bled his life away. But for those in his community who knew him, the only explanation that was needed was that his time had come.

46

"*T*rust me, I know. He will be dining at the Palffy Palace, just outside the gates of Prague Castle. If we hurry, we can get there before his *Uzené* is served." Despite the brevity of their fling, Camille had come to know Emil's eating habits; which included a strange taste for that beloved Czech specialty, smoked pork with slices of potato dumpling accompanied by globs of white sauerkraut. (It helps if you're Czech.)

They all crowded into the same taxi: Camille, Zinka, Bertie, Pino and Brocard. Were they not extremely close friends, it would have been an insufferable ride. As it was, they used the time to catch up on where they were. Or weren't.

None of them were particularly in the mood to talk, as each in their own way had felt they had been let down or, at worst, deceived. However, Brocard knew that much had already been accomplished and decided to break the silence by commending Bertie.

"Spare me your backhanded compliments, Brocard, please," Bertie said, cutting Brocard off in mid-sentence. I was wrong about Otger, there I said it, wrong. Pleased?"

"My dear Father Bertram," then realizing he would do better being less formal, "Bertie, I mean, Otger was indeed part of the operation, just not the master mind you thought him to be. A perfectly understandable mistake that has done no harm."

"In fact," Camille said slapping Pino's hand as he fixed it firmly on her thigh, "thanks to your quick thinking Bertie, a great deal of the art is in Interpol's hands."

"Well I guess it was pretty clever of me to tell those two cops to tail the trucks Otger was packing up so as to discover the warehouse that was being used," Bertie admitted. Yes, he thought, the mystery was more about the art than gaining personal satisfaction at bringing down his old nemesis Father Otger Deblaer. He should feel proud.

"It was funny to watch your face though," Pino said to Bertie, tactful as ever, "when the warehouse custodian told you that Natalia had the key, not Otger." Here Pino started to laugh and point his finger like a malicious brat. Hurt, Bertie quickly recovered.

"Oh don't be silly," Bertie said giving his lover a slap. Even when thoroughly obnoxious, Bertie found Pino engaging. "We helped win the day, don't you see? Even Brocard has said it. You and me Pino, the brains and brawn so to speak, we did it."

Zinka was seated in the front passenger seat, solitary and unusually silent. No one could tell if she was brooding over the loss of the Church of Doom, the loss of her sister, or both. Thinking that she might be grieving, the pastoral side of Brocard came out. He took out his handkerchief, just in case it would be needed, and placed his hand gently on her back. "Zinka," he said in his most compassionate tone. "Zinka how are you doing?"

"Oh Christ, I hate it when you get all priestly. Just cut the crap, Brocard, please."

Then turning, Zinka showed that she was in no way distressed. On the contrary, she looked radiantly composed. "What a lark, don't you think? Recovered art, new age spirituality and a family reunion all rolled up in one. A good time was had by all, no?"

No one knew quite what to say. Finally, Camille, who arguably knew her girlfriend better than all the others, ventured a reply. "Zinka, my dear, what about the people who died, the suicides and those buried under that horrid mountain of mud?"

"Oh pooh, Camille, you can be such a pious prig." Zinka reached back to take her hand but just then the taxi went over a bump and Zinka's great paw landed in Pino's groin. "Sorry," she said giving him a little wink and a squeeze before taking hold of Camille's hand. "Now Camille please, don't spoil all of our fun. Don't be a pooper please."

Brocard was not sure of the use of 'pooper' alone. Party pooper yes, but pooper, he was not sure about that. Thinking it best not to default into his pedantic mode, Brocard decided to ask Zinka the question all of them wanted answered but which no one had the courage to ask.

"Where is Natalia, Zinka?" Brocard demanded in a clear, forthright voice that demanded a reply, "We all saw you leave the Hall with her, so where is she?"

"Well haven't you become a demanding little monk," Zinka said, her face betraying nothing. "She's dead, of course, my poor beautiful sister Natalia. Quite dead." Here Zinka reached for the handkerchief in Brocard's hand and used it to dab the corners of her eyes, even though they were as dry as a Methodist on Sunday. "Those beautiful eyes, that exquisite complexion—not to mention those tits—all covered over by mud. I tried to save her, of course, but she wouldn't hear of it. Her faith was strong, so strong you know. I take comfort in the fact that she is on the Mother Ship now, sailing out into infinity." Seeing that her companions didn't know what to do with this information, Zinka sighed then sighed again, as if to say, it's over, that's all you're getting from me. Gratefully, they got the message because it was very hard for her to do sad lies. Happy lies were her forte—she could weave them for hours; sad ones took a great deal out of her.

The taxi screeched to a halt in front of the Palffy Palace, an eighteenth century pile that housed a restaurant favored by those who like traditional Czech food and music. Camille, the only fiscally reliable one of the lot, paid the fare and they rushed down a dank staircase into the main dining room. There at a far table, alone and content, sat Emil.

As none of the others except Brocard knew why on earth they had so dramatically descended on Dr. Emil Rothenberg, they followed his lead. Fortunately there were few other patrons in the restaurant so the disturbance they made was minimal. The confusion caused to Emil, however, the terror etched on his face, more than compensated, ratcheting the emotional atmosphere up to a fevered pitch.

"You." Emil said putting down his fork. "How did you know?"

"Let's just say, a lady who died a few centuries ago told me," Brocard said bearing down on Emil, deciding it was better for him to stand than take seat at table.

"You always were a strange one, Father Brocard. But I never did think you very clever—until now, that is." Emil had regained his composure enough to take another bite of his *Uzené.* "I would want this to get cold," he said, refusing to offer any of them a bite.

"When did it start, Emil, that is what I want to know," Brocard prodded him.

"Natalia's husband and I were old, old friends. School friends in fact. He had a love for art and being Czech, was the one who introduced me to the glories of the Bohemian Baroque. When his wife began hallucinating—that's what we both thought and I still do, hallucinating—he saw a way of marketing this, he was a businessman after all and New Age was becoming all the rage in Eastern Europe after the fall of Communism. I like to think of it as their spiritual illiteracy, you know. Like children really that didn't know any better." Emil paused to savour another mouthful and then signalled for Brocard or any of them to take a seat at his empty table. Zinka, of course, plopped herself down. Brocard decided he was in a stronger position, as interrogator, standing.

"So you used her, is that what happened? Got her to lure unsuspecting souls to her cult. But how did you target those who had access to art?"

"Church rats are the easiest types to dupe, Father Brocard,

surely you know that? And in the Bohemian countryside, where there were few if any priests during the communist years, the sacristans and custodians took ownership of their churches and all of the objects in them. And these same poor souls were the ones most likely to be attracted to the message the Church of the Age of Doom offered. A clear message, no equivocating, with a clear reward. That's what they longed for after so many years of uncertainty. Simple answer; assured rewards."

"Otger, what about Otger," Bertie asked. "How did he fit in?"

"I invited him, of course, because it was not fitting for me to do the hard work of cataloguing and transporting.   We   knew each other over the years, Dr. Aarnack and I. His expertise and amenability were well known. For a price, Otger could be counted on."

A righteous indignation had seized Brocard. The arrogance of this pig, he thought, stuffing his face while others lie buried, while lives have been destroyed and for what? "For what purpose," Brocard blurted out, "what in God's name did you hope to achieve?"

"In God's name, nothing," Emil said refusing to lay down his fork, piling the food in him incessantly. Speaking, to Brocard's complete and utter distain, with his mouth full. "In my name, everything." Emil seemed like a man possessed, which indeed he was. And he would not, could not be stopped. Words tumbled out as rapidly as food was piled in.

"To dictate how people see, the way in which history is written — don't you see how glorious that is? The whole area of Bohemian Baroque is the last, great unknown waiting to be conquered. Needing to be controlled. And I, Emil Rothenberg, held the key. Not just the knowledge, that I always had, but I now know where the paintings were. Everything of significance, from catalogue raisonnes to auctions, everything was under my control. And there was no stopping me. But it was not about money, no nothing so petty could interest me. It was and is all about power, the power to dictate taste, the power to determine what people think…".

There were no more words, in the silence that followed all

that could be heard was a gagging sound coming from Emil, as he grasped at his throat. Zinka considered picking him up by his feet, flipping him over and giving him a pat on the back to dislodge the food. But, large as she was, she just as quickly abandoned this notion. Brocard wondered if the Blessing of Throats of St. Blaise had any effect outside his Feast Day; and decided it probably did not. Pino, ever fascinated by the bizarre, was entranced by the color purple Emil had turned. Camille, who had been truly engaged by Emil's diabolic screed, rather hoped he would cough up whatever it was and get on with his story. Still, she was prepared for the worst, as she knew that the fat die young. And the Maitre D', intent that he would not lose a patron on his watch, scrambled around madly looking for the card with the Heimlich Maneuver on it, the one that was supposed to be posted in full view. But it was too late. Dr.Emil Rothenberg fell over into his own vomit and died.

As deaths go Emil's was reasonably calm. There he lay in a pool of undigested slices of potato dumpling and globs of white sauerkraut. Except for the smell, his demise was relatively dignified as appropriate for someone of his breeding.

After the ambulance had collected the body and the police had made their report, Zinka and Company decided to have lunch. In truth, they had all worked up quite an appetite over this whole affair. Except for *Uzené*, they were ready to eat anything.

It was the ever-impetuous Bertie who broke the silence that had descended upon them. He wondered what mystery they would be solving next, knowing full well how indispensable he now was. Where it would call them and what art they would have to recover. Brocard, weary to the bone, said that he did not have the energy for another.

Zinka, for once, couldn't have agreed more.

Epilogue

*R*arely had there been a burial as beautiful as Avertanus's was. Even the weather obliged—cloudless, air crisp and fresh. Not to mention the flowers in full bloom, their riotous colors attracting a profusion of birds and butterflies.

It was the mourners, however, who made it all so right. No one that was there did not respect and love this old man, who had touched each of their lives uniquely. Of course he was loopy, Avertanus. But so benign, so caring and so empathetic, that his eccentricity was merely part of his charm.

What a varied lot they were, as they gathered around the gravesite. In the first rank was the Prior Provincial, who had flown in from Rome, and the local Provincial of the community in Zenderen. Behind them stood fellow brothers from the Order, those at least who were ambulatory enough to make it down from their cells. The others watched from the second floor windows, attentive and moved.

At the foot of the coffin were his friends, lined in semi-circle. Bertie pointed out Appolonia's hermitage, just beyond the trees barely visible above the cloister walls, to Pino. To his great relief, Pino shrugged this information off and tightened his strong arm around Bertie's shoulder. The past, he said without having to utter a word, was over and forgotten. They had been through so much; grown so much together.

Zinka wore black. Tasteful as her ensemble was, Camille thought that, given the occasion, the cleavage was a bit much. So in the limousine, she had taken one of her handkerchief and lovingly arranged it to cover the offending skin. "What a lucky girl I am to have you, my little pumpkin," Zinka told her. "Me too," Camille agreed. "Me too."

Throughout the committal Brocard held the ancient tome of Avertanus under his arm. He brought it out of respect, fully aware that there was no way that he could use it—not a chance that he could become the Magus that Avertanus had thought he might be. The wisdom and intellectual curiosity of Avertanus could not be so easily passed on, at least to him. Brocard's was a more simple learning, less scholarly and without pretense. Before leaving Zenderen he planned to deposit the *Conclusiones Magicae*, complete with Avertanus's years of annotations, in the community library. Hopefully another soul, perhaps unborn, capable of unraveling its mysteries would stumble across it and unlock its wisdom. As for Brocard, he planned to retire quietly to the Mount, far from New Age Communes and Mafia Dons, International Art Thefts and their attendant corpses. Or that, at least, is what he so fervently prayed for, to a God who had never once abandoned him, had not once let him down.

The others understood that he wanted to be alone, once a monk always a monk. After saying his good-byes late in the day, Brocard walked out into the fields. There was no rush for him to get to the station or anywhere in fact.

It was there in that open space, away from everything and everyone, that he felt God's presence more than he ever had before. Years of self-denial and disciplined religious life had not prepared him for this one moment. The sensation that came over him was one of being held; an indescribable feeling of being accepted, fully loved and at peace. And the words that came to him in the wake of this experience were the words attributed to Mary, the words of the *Magnificat* that he said every night in Evening Prayer. My soul glorifies the Lord, My spirit gives thanks to God my savior.

How often over the past few years had he been confronted with evil, raw and diabolic, and come through? How many times had he faced death, in flood or fire or mudslide, and lived, so that the truth of those horrible, corrupt systems might be told.

Suddenly everything made sense. All the adventure and mishaps that he and Zinka and Bertie and all of them had been through for the past ten years finally made sense. The truth lay imbedded in one line of that timeworn prayer:

He has lifted up the lowly; the mighty He has brought down from their thrones.

Who were the lowly if not the sinners, the prostitutes, the outcastes? And who were the mighty if not those in religion, in the state and in the arts who abuse their authority? Who were the mighty if not those who were so desperate to keep their power that their lives were driven by hatred and exclusion? To manipulate others as if they were objects on a chessboard, to strip them of their dignity, was loathsome. To condemn someone for their sexuality — for whom they love — was a sick little human game. Hardly God's plan.

The beauty of the wonderful Poussin painting that started them on this remarkable journey came back to him — Agatha herself, as vulnerable as she was timeless. And with her came a flood of images that brought a smile to his face: crazy Zinka and her band of merry players, mixing humor with a steely determination to get to the truth. Obsession was part of it, of course; and sometimes things had gotten positively manic. But there was so much life in it — such life.

www.ingramcontent.com/pod-product-compliance
Lightning Source LLC
Chambersburg PA
CBHW030132260626
47156CB00008B/2902